I0591844

Monster Makers

Book, Music & Lyrics by
Stephen Dolginoff

A SAMUEL FRENCH ACTING EDITION

SAMUEL
FRENCH
FOUNDED 1830

SAMUELFRENCH.COM
SAMUELFRENCH-LONDON.CO.UK

FOR PRODUCTION ENQUIRIES

UNITED STATES AND CANADA
Info@SamuelFrench.com
1-866-598-8449

UNITED KINGDOM AND EUROPE
Plays@SamuelFrench-London.co.uk
020-7255-4302

Each title is subject to availability from Samuel French, depending upon
country of performance. Please be aware that MONSTER MAKERS may
not be licensed by Samuel French in your territory. Professional and
amateur producers should contact the nearest Samuel French office or
licensing partner to verify availability.

MUSIC USE NOTE

Licensees are solely responsible for obtaining formal written permission from copyright owners to use copyrighted music in the performance of this play and are strongly cautioned to do so. If no such permission is obtained by the licensee, then the licensee must use only original music that the licensee owns and controls. Licensees are solely responsible and liable for all music clearances and shall indemnify the copyright owners of the play(s) and their licensing agent, Samuel French, against any costs, expenses, losses and liabilities arising from the use of music by licensees. Please contact the appropriate music licensing authority in your territory for the rights to any incidental music.

RENTAL MATERIALS

A rental package consisting of **Piano/Conductor Score and five (5) Vocal/ Chorus Books** will be loaned two months prior to the production ONLY on the receipt of the Licensing Fee quoted for all performances, the rental fee and a refundable deposit. Please contact Samuel French for perusal of the music materials as well as a performance license application.

IMPORTANT BILLING AND CREDIT REQUIREMENTS

If you have obtained performance rights to this title, please refer to your licensing agreement for important billing and credit requirements.

MONSTER MAKERS was first presented as a concert version at the Daryl Roth Theatre/D-Lounge in New York City on June 22, 2015. It was produced by New York Theatre Barn (Joe Barros, Artistic Director; Mark Montague, Managing Director; Laura Brandel, Artistic Producer). The performers were Stephen Dolginoff, Camille Diamond, John McVeigh, Leo Ash Evens, and Zachary Orts.

MONSTER MAKERS was subsequently produced at LAMB Arts Regional Theatre in Sioux City, Iowa (Russell Wooley, Managing/Artistic Director/Producer; Diana Wooley, Producer), on September 25, 2015. The director was Russell Wooley with musical direction by Donald E. Short III, scenic design by Tim Case, sound design by Russell Wooley, lighting design by Michael Rohlena, costume design by Karen Sowienski, properties by Alyssa Collett, and piano arrangements by Zachary Orts and Stephen Dolginoff. The stage manager was Jaden Groves. The cast was as follows:

MURNAU/WHALE/FISHER . . . . Michael Powell

PIERCE/MORITZ/STUNTMAN . . . . Donny Short

PETER/MAX/KARLOFF . . . . Matt Cihak

ALBIN/CARL/HINDS . . . . Brian Hamman

MRS. STOKER/VERA/VICTORIA. .Jessica Wheeler

CAST

ACTOR ONE........................ **F.W. MURNAU; JAMES WHALE; TERENCE FISHER** *(Directors)*

ACTOR TWO............................. **MORITZ; JACK PIERCE; DRACULA'S STUNTMAN** *(Various Men)*

ACTOR THREE.................. **MAX SCHRECK; BORIS KARLOFF; PETER CUSHING** *(Actors)*

ACTOR FOUR..................... **ALBIN GRAU; CARL LAEMMLE; ANTHONY HINDS** *(Producers)*

ACTOR FIVE .... **MRS. STOKER; VERA WEST; VICTORIA** *(Women)*

CHARACTER DESCRIPTIONS

ACT ONE
F.W. MURNAU – a flamboyant director
ALBIN GRAU – a stern producer
MORITZ – a meek lawyer
MAX SCHRECK – a creepy actor
MRS. FLORENCE STOKER – a formidable widow

ACT TWO
JACK PIERCE – a maniacal make-up artist
JAMES WHALE – a well-mannered director
BORIS KARLOFF – a friendly actor
CARL LAEMMLE – a typical Hollywood producer
VERA WEST – a wisecracking costume designer

ACT THREE
PETER CUSHING – a dignified movie star
DRACULA'S STUNTMAN – a nonchalant guy
TERENCE FISHER – a petulant director
ANTHONY HINDS – a jovial producer
VICTORIA – a sexy actress

*MONSTER MAKERS is an unauthorized parody,
based on facts in the public domain.*

MUSICAL NUMBERS

PROLOGUE: "COMING ATTRACTIONS"

"OPENING" *(Murnau, Pierce, Peter)*

ACT ONE: "OUT FOR BLOOD"
(A courthouse in Germany, 1922)

"SACRIFICE MY VISION" *(Murnau)*

"THE NIGHT WE FILMED YOUR DEATH" *(Murnau and Max)*

"OUT FOR BLOOD" *(Mrs. Stoker)*

REPRISE: "SACRIFICE MY VISION" *(Murnau)*

ACT TWO: "I'VE CREATED A MONSTER"
(A make-up room in Hollywood, 1931)

"CREATING A MONSTER" *(Pierce and Karloff)*

REPRISE: "CREATING A MONSTER" *(Whale, Vera, Pierce and Karloff)*

"I WANT IT MY WAY" *(Whale)*

"TAKE THE WORLD BY STORM" *(Pierce)*

ACT THREE: "THE FINAL NAIL IN THE COFFIN"
(A film studio in England, 1973)

"NEVER LET THE PERFECT BE THE ENEMY OF THE GOOD" *(Peter)*

"NAIL IN THE COFFIN" *(Peter and Fisher)*

"HORROR FAN" *(Victoria)*

REPRISE: "NAIL IN THE COFFIN" *(Peter)*

EPILOGUE: "THE END!?"

"FINALE" *(Peter, Pierce, Murnau)*

***MONSTER MAKERS** is performed without an intermission.*

AUTHOR'S NOTES

Along with writing and composing, horror movies have been one of my greatest passions since I was very young. I grew up watching weekend classic monster movie marathons, reading *Famous Monsters of Filmland* magazines and building and painting iconic Aurora plastic monster model kits. **MONSTER MAKERS** is a loving tribute to these wonderful films and the creative geniuses behind them – many of whom never got the credit they truly deserved in their own lifetimes.

Each act of **MONSTER MAKERS** is inspired by a true story and is presented onstage as a parody of the style of the horror movie that is being referenced. Performed seamlessly, without an intermission, the show should run 90-100 minutes. Act One is presented as a parody of the exaggerated, shadowy, melodramatic style of a silent-film from the German-Expressionist era. It's as if flamboyant F.W. Murnau is trapped in a silent horror movie nightmare of his own making. Designed in sepia tones and heavy shadows. Act Two is presented as a parody of the classic 1930s Universal Studios monster movies, with a thunderstorm constantly raging outside. It's as if Jack Pierce is a giddy mad-scientist, like Dr. Frankenstein himself, in his make-up room that looks like a laboratory. Designed in stark black & white. Act Three is presented as a parody of the over-the-top, low-budget color British horror films made by Hammer Studios in the 1970s. It's as if dignified actor Peter Cushing is re-experiencing the entire history of Hammer Studios all on the final day of filming. Designed in blood-drenched color.

It is also possible to do **MONSTER MAKERS** very simply with minimal scenery. It could be performed in a black box with only the costumes in the various suggested color schemes, or perhaps in front of a movie screen with film-like images projected as scenery.

Five actors perform all of the characters. Making each role distinct, perhaps with a different accent, is crucial. If necessary, the roles can be divided up differently between the actors then the way they are described in the text. But it is strongly recommended to use the preferred approach, which is coordinated with the script to account for costume changes and creates specific arcs for each performer. Actor Four (the producers) is conceived as a non-singing role. If that is not desirable, a switch can be made: Actor One can portray Anthony Hinds, and Actor Four can play Terence Fisher. Some groups may wish to expand to a cast of fifteen actors, or some other variation, but a cast of five is suggested.

It is important for me to point out that F.W. Murnau's silent film *Nosferatu*, Bram Stoker's novel *Dracula* and Mary Shelley's novel *Frankenstein* are all in the public domain. However, all films made by Hammer, all of Universal's *Frankenstein* movies, the original *Frankenstein* make-up design and the actual image of Boris Karloff in or out of make-up, all remain under copyright and/or trademark protection. No photos, clips, dialogue, artwork, or any other aspect of this protected material may be used in a production of *MONSTER MAKERS*, or as part of any publicity.

There are plenty of resources available to research all of these wonderful performers, directors, designers, producers and the movies they made. But remember, *MONSTER MAKERS* is a parody inspired by history and has been filtered through my imagination. Have a frighteningly good time!

– Stephen Dolginoff

AUTHOR'S ACKNOWLEDGEMENTS

Special thanks to Zachary Orts (piano arrangements), Ed Garrison, Jason Rockwood, Chip Fabrizi, Doug Kreeger, Joe Barros, Linda Weilkotz, Craig Tiede, Evan T. Charpentier, Old Library Theatre, Nicole Del Percio, Seth Arrobas, Frankie Rowles, Chad Parsons, Russ and Diana Wooley, Donny Short, Paul Graham Brown, Moritz Staemmler, Amy Wagner, Ron Gwiazda, Bob Hamilton, Amy Rose Marsh, Ben Coleman, David Geer, Tyler Mullen, Chris Kam and the entire Samuel French team.

PROLOGUE
"COMING ATTRACTIONS"

(A crash of thunder and lightning plunges the house into complete darkness. A spooky overture begins.)

[MUSIC NO. 1 – "OVERTURE"]

(Three separate pools of light find **F.W. MURNAU**, **JACK PIERCE** *and* **PETER CUSHING**, *all of whom we will meet later. For now, they simply stand in place, each posed as if depicted on their own enticing monster movie poster. Each wears a distinct costume:* **MURNAU** *in sepia;* **PIERCE** *in black & white;* **CUSHING** *in rich color. They each sing a single line of their own theme which we will hear fully as the individual stories later unfold.)*

[MUSIC NO. 2 – "OPENING"]

F.W. MURNAU. *(heartfelt)*
I WON'T SACRIFICE MY VISION...

    (He strikes a melodramatic 'silent movie' pose.)

JACK PIERCE. *(gleeful)*
WHEN I'M CREATING A MONSTER,
I MUST GIVE THE MONSTER RESPECT...

    (He laughs maniacally.)

PETER CUSHING. *(kindly)*
I NEVER LET THE PERFECT
BE THE ENEMY OF THE GOOD...

    (He stands majestically, like a true star.

    The music crescendos. The three men gradually disappear, leaving the stage completely dark and seemingly empty as the music continues...)

ACT ONE
"OUT FOR BLOOD"

Germany, 1922.
A Laywer's Conference Room In A Courthouse

(The music subsides to allow for a few brief moments of deliberate silence. A flickering light, as if from a film projector, gradually reveals a lawyer's conference room in an old, oppressive courthouse. It is styled to look like a stark, German expressionist film. There are deliberately exaggerated, sharp and unusual angles; heavy, dark, imposing shadows; and an overall moody, sense-of-doom quality. Everything is in sepia tones, including the costumes.

In the center of the room is a small conference table with a few wooden chairs. And on one side stands a large, creaky door that looks like it belongs in a haunted house. [If the door is difficult to achieve, entrances can be made from the wings, perhaps with extra sound and shadow effects to compensate.]

F.W. MURNAU [*Actor One*], *a flamboyant, over-dramatic man in his 30s, is slowly revealed, first in shadow. He hasn't slept in days. There are circles under his eyes, his clothing is rumpled, his hair is a mess, his skin is pale – giving it the look of 'silent movie' make-up. He sits alone in silence. Suddenly the large creaky door starts to open ever so slowly, casting a thin shaft of blinding light across the stage.* **MURNAU** *seems terrified of what's behind the door. 'Silent movie' music begins.)*

[MUSIC NO. 3 – "SILENT MOVIE NIGHTMARE UNDERSCORE"]

(With a chilling echo that sounds like something out of a horror movie, a SCARY VOICE is heard from behind the door.)

SCARY VOICE (ALBIN). I *warned* you...

MURNAU. No!

(MURNAU can't stand to listen. He covers his ears with his hands. The lights begin swirling around him, like some sort of hypnotic, nightmare sequence. The voice grows louder, as the door creaks open slightly more.)

SCARY VOICE (ALBIN). I *warned* you...

MURNAU. Stop!

(MURNAU keeps sweating, panicking, and trying to ignore the nightmarish voice that seems to be ringing through his head. Music continues as the shadow of an outstretched arm with its hand pointing at MURNAU emerges from behind the door. As in Nosferatu, *it is only the shadow we see – not the arm itself – yet.)*

SCARY VOICE (ALBIN). I *warned* you...

MURNAU. Please!

(The shadow of the hand is practically touching MURNAU, almost clawing at him. Not being able to stand it any longer, he backs away, petrified.)

SCARY VOICE (ALBIN). I *warned* you...

MURNAU. *(screaming)* Let this nightmare end!!!

(The door opens completely, to reveal the man behind the voice and the shadow. It is ALBIN GRAU [Actor Four], a stern man in his late 30s. Immediately the music stops and the surreal nightmare effect ends.)

ALBIN. I warned you, Freddy.

MURNAU. I can't listen anymore!

ALBIN. Well, you're going to have to listen because I'm going to keep saying it. I warned you this would happen, I told you how it could all be avoided.

MURNAU. Albin, you're a producer, not an artist.

ALBIN. Fortunately.

MURNAU. How is it unfolding in the courtroom?

ALBIN. You'd find out if you went inside.

> *(Remember the melodramatic 'silent movie' gestures!)*

MURNAU. I cannot sit there while a judge decides the fate of my creation...after that damned Stoker lawyer distorted everything I said.

ALBIN. How rude he was. It was almost as if he was cross-examining a man who stole someone else's book without permission.

MURNAU. Stop it! If Moritz just did his job in there...

ALBIN. Moritz is the most inexperienced lawyer in Germany.

MURNAU. And also the cheapest.

ALBIN. All screenings are cancelled until the trial is over. If we can't exhibit the film, we can't make any money, Herr Director.

MURNAU. Money means nothing to me!

ALBIN. You are dead-set on giving me a heart-attack, aren't you?

> *(MURNAU dramatically scoffs.)*

There's only one *Dracula*. And sadly, Frau Stoker owns him.

MURNAU. Don't call her "Frau" – no fellow German would put me through this. It's *Mrs.* Stoker!

ALBIN. Of course.

MURNAU. And there is no "Dracula" in *Nosferatu*.

ALBIN. Freddy, I'm not the judge, you don't have to sell me the propaganda.

MURNAU. You can't copyright a generic vampire! They are creatures of the public domain.

ALBIN. You changed the title and the names, the rest was pure Bram Stoker.

MURNAU. *We* changed the names, Herr. Producer. And it wouldn't have been necessary if you'd gotten us the rights in the first place.

ALBIN. I tried. You know I tried.

MURNAU. Not hard enough. Now look at where we are. Wasting what is sure to be the greatest horror film in the history of German cinema.

ALBIN. Well, if your friend Fritz Lang finally gets that *Metropolis* thing off the ground...

MURNAU. *(offended)* Please! That will be *science fiction*!

ALBIN. I said I would finance whatever you wanted to make. It didn't *have* to be this *Dracula*...

> (**MURNAU** *shoots him a look.*)

Sorry...this *vampire* movie.

MURNAU. I told you I'm an *artist*. I had a calling...an image for this film like nothing I've ever had before. There was no choice for me. It had to be captured on celluloid and unspooled for the world...

ALBIN. All right, all right! I get it. But if you'd just made *all* of the changes that I suggested during filming...

MURNAU. Changes!? You mean distortions! How many times do I have to remind you, Albin?

> *(Music begins.)*

> *[MUSIC NO. 4 – "SACRIFICE MY VISION"]*

> *(Remember the melodramatic 'silent movie' gestures!)*

I WON'T
SACRIFICE MY VISION
NO MATTER WHO THE DEMONS ARE
THAT I MAY HAVE TO FIGHT.
I'LL DEFEND
EACH ARTISTIC FILM DECISION
IT'S THE ONLY WAY

> THAT I CAN SLEEP AT NIGHT.
> AND I'M HOPEFUL THAT THE JUDGE
> WILL SEE THE LIGHT!

> *(Music continues.)*

ALBIN. Maybe we can make some alterations to the prints – cut in new title cards – rearrange some scenes...film a few new ones.

MURNAU. Now you've *really* lost your mind...

> *(He sings.)*

> I WON'T
> COMPROMISE OR EDIT
> NO MATTER WHO IS ASKING
> EVEN IF IT'S ONLY YOU.
> IGNORE THAT NOVEL,
> I'LL DENY I EVER READ IT
> MY ART CANNOT BE
> UNDERMINED, IT'S TRUE
> AND I WON'T CHANGE A FRAME
> THE FILM IS *THROUGH*!

> *(Music continues.)*

ALBIN. We need to have a contingency. Something to offer Frau... *Mrs.* Stoker.

MURNAU.

> I WON'T
> BARGAIN WITH THE DEVIL
> NO MATTER WHAT THE QUESTION IS
> NO DIFFERENCE WHO IT'S FOR
> I REFUSE
> TO SINK TO THAT LOW LEVEL
> IT'S MY POLICY
> TO NOT WALK THROUGH THAT DOOR
> AND MY CREATIVE SOUL
> CAN'T TAKE THIS
> ANYMORE!

> I'LL LET SOME COWARD CHANGE HIS MIND
> AND LEAVE INTEGRITY BEHIND

I'LL LET SOME QUITTER
HAVE RELUCTANCY TO FIGHT
BUT IF WE'RE TALKING ABOUT ME
IT'S SO OBVIOUS TO SEE
THAT I'LL ALWAYS TAKE THE VIEWPOINT
THAT I'M RIGHT!

AND I WON'T
SACRIFICE MY VISION
I MUST PROTECT THE PATRONS
AT OUR CINEMATIC SHOW.
I WORK
WITH PAINSTAKING PRECISION
AND I WON'T ADJUST MY METHODS
OR LET GO.
SINCE MY LEGACY'S IMPORTANT,
AS YOU KNOW
MY WHOLE LIFE IS THERE
IN EACH PROJECTOR'S GLOW
WHEN I'M ASKED FOR A CONCESSION
I'LL ALWAYS SAY NO!

> *(The song ends with a flourish.)*

ALBIN. I wish you could make a film out of yourself right now, Freddy. The story of a desperate man saying crazy things.

MURNAU. I have to keep hope alive.

> *[MUSIC NO. 5 – "SILENT MOVIE UNDERSCORE" – MORITZ ENTRANCE.]*

> *(Music begins as the door creaks open again, revealing the scary shadow of a small-statured, hunched-over figure. From the posture, it looks like some sort of creature. **MURNAU** clutches **ALBIN** out of fear as they watch the door. Finally the shadow is revealed to be **MORITZ**, the lawyer [Actor Two], a fragile, nervous man whose nose is buried in a legal brief.)*

MORITZ. We're dead.

ALBIN. What the devil are you talking about, Moritz? And shouldn't you be in there defending us?

(**MORITZ** *recoils as if horribly frightened of* **ALBIN**.)

MORITZ. I'm sorry Herr Grau. I begged for a short recess. I just received this subpoena from the Stoker estate. They're demanding a mimeograph of the screenplay.

ALBIN. That's what I was afraid of.

(*Remember the melodramatic 'silent movie' gestures!*)

MURNAU. I disposed of mine, as you forced me to do!

ALBIN. So did I. And the actors only received their necessary pages. I made sure no one got a complete script.

MORITZ. Thank goodness. Otherwise we'd be slaughtered in there. But as long as there aren't any existing duplicates to give them...

MURNAU. Well...that may not be the case.

[MUSIC NO. 6 – STING CUES]

(*Underscore "sting."*)

ALBIN. What do you mean?

MURNAU. Max.

MORITZ. *(panicked)* Max Schrek? The star of the movie? Count Dracula himself?

MURNAU. *(frustrated)* Count *Orlock*!

(**MORITZ** *recoils.*)

ALBIN. I never gave him a script.

MURNAU. *(ashamed)* I did.

(*Underscore bigger "sting."*)

MORITZ. Oh, dear.

(**MURNAU** *and* **ALBIN** *both give* **MORITZ** *evil-eyed looks. He shirks in fear.*)

ALBIN. What possessed you to do that?

MURNAU. He was so perfect for the vampire part, but he wasn't sure he wanted to do it. I had to let him read the whole thing before he would agree.

ALBIN. *(disgusted)* Actors!

MORITZ. I'm so sorry, Herr Murnau, Herr Grau. But Herr Shreck is in the courtroom now, and he'll be testifying soon. I'm terrified to ask...but...did he *keep* the script?

MURNAU. He brought it with him today.

> *(An even bigger underscore "sting.")*

ALBIN. What?

> **(MORITZ** *reacts as if he's just been given a death sentence.)*

MORITZ. You...you mean...he...he has it with him *now?*

MURNAU. Yes.

ALBIN. But why, Freddy?

MURNAU. He was going to give it back to me.

ALBIN. Oh, no. Are you insane?

MURNAU. I deserve to have one for my archives, Albin.

> **(MORITZ** *starts pleading hysterically.)*

MORITZ. Herr Grau, it will be the first question the judge asks him. And if they get their hands on that screenplay it'll ruin our whole case...we'll have no leg left to stand on. Frau Stoker will have all she needs...

> **(ALBIN** *grabs him.)*

ALBIN. Moritz, calm down. You're upsetting Herr Murnau. And he's a delicate artist.

MORITZ. I'm sorry, sir.

ALBIN. You'll have to make sure none of that happens.

MORITZ. *(frightened)* I'm... I'm not sure I can do that...

MURNAU. *(scoffs)* Lawyers are even worse than producers!

ALBIN. How do you think it's going otherwise?

MORITZ. I... I think the judge appreciates that the characters aren't *exactly* the same.

MURNAU. Then there's still hope.

MORITZ. *(shaking)* Until Frau Stoker sees that screenplay. And she's a very formidable woman. I'm so scared of how she'll talk to me from the witness stand.

(**ALBIN** *stares him down and moves in even closer.*)

ALBIN. *(sternly)* Just get back in there.

MORITZ. Yes, sir.

ALBIN. Now!

[*MUSIC NO. 7 – MORITZ EXIT*]

(*Dramatic underscore music begins.* **MORITZ** *scurries to the door like a frightened animal, but he is so nervous that he can hardly open it. The door creaks and creaks.*)

MORITZ. *(begging)* Won't someone help me, please?

(**MURNAU** *and* **ALBIN** *just watch as* **MORITZ** *finally makes it through the door. It loudly slams behind him.*)

MURNAU. I just love watching him squirm.

ALBIN. Well, Freddy, that's that. It's the end of both of our careers, because you just had to have a memento of this miserable ordeal!

MURNAU. Stop being so dramatic, Albin.

ALBIN. *I'm* being dramatic?

MURNAU. I can talk to Max. We just need to convince him to tell the court he never had the script.

ALBIN. You think that *actor* will lie for you?

MURNAU. I'll tell him it's an audition for a role.

ALBIN. Please, Freddy, you have to take this seriously.

MURNAU. What do you want me to say to him, Herr Producer?

ALBIN. Just get that script back and tear it up. Or burn it.

(*Remember the melodramatic 'silent movie' gestures!*)

MURNAU. Over my dead body. It's my legacy.

ALBIN. You are truly a madman. It's the evidence to ruin you.

MURNAU. Albin, give it to me straight. What's the worst that can happen if we lose?

ALBIN. We'd probably have to give Bram Stoker credit...

MURNAU. I'd rather drink poison...

ALBIN. ...and pay the estate a huge royalty.

MURNAU. That's not so bad.

ALBIN. Prana films can't afford to pay *anything*. Or lose any part of the profits. If there ever are any.

MURNAU. There will be! Audiences will line up...

ALBIN. There may never be another audience. We could be forbidden from ever exhibiting it again.

MURNAU. People will demand to see it! The *critics* say it's a triumph. *My* triumph. And that's the most important thing –

ALBIN. Then let the critics pay you. And let the critics defend you. That script *cannot exist.*

MURNAU. You'd better get Max in here, then. Before the recess is over.

> (**ALBIN** *goes to the heavy door and opens it with an ominous creak.*)

ALBIN. And you'd better hope he takes direction well.

> [*MUSIC NO. 8 – "SACRIFICE" - SUNG TAG & UNDERSCORE*]

> (*Music begins as* **ALBIN** *exits.* **MURNAU** *drops his guard and slowly sings.*)

MURNAU.
I WON'T
SACRIFICE MY VISION
NO MATTER HOW MUCH SWEAT
MAY BE APPARENT ON MY BROW.
ALTHOUGH I MIGHT
BE HEADED FOR COLLISION
I'LL NEVER SHOW A WEAKNESS –
DON'T KNOW HOW.
MY FATE IN SOMEONE ELSE'S HANDS –
I WON'T ALLOW.

(*The door creaks open, casting the silhouette of* **MAX SCHRECK** [Actor Three] *across the room. The exaggerated shadow of both his arms reach toward* **MURNAU** *as if attempting to strangle him. His voice is heard in eerie echo, calling to* **MURNAU**.)

MAX'S VOICE. (*in echo*) Come here…

(**MURNAU** *seems terrified again as the voice rings through his head. It's like he is being tortured. The nightmarish lights again swirl around him.*)

(*in echo*) Come here…

(**MURNAU** *can't take it anymore.*)

MURNAU. Stop! Please stop!

(*The nightmarish echo, music and lighting end. Finally* **MAX**, *a creepy "Igor" type-man in his 30s, who has a voice perfect for silent movies, is revealed in person, with his arms outstretched for a hug.*)

MAX. Come here, you poor, poor thing. Give Max a hug.

(*He goes to* **MURNAU** *and gives him a warm, friendly hug.*)

This is all just dreadful. Ghastly.

MURNAU. Thank you, Max. You're a real class act.

MAX. How are you holding up, Freddy?

MURNAU. I'm hanging in there.

MAX. Those barbarians just don't understand art, do they?

MURNAU. They most certainly do not.

(**MAX** *reaches into his messenger bag.*)

MAX. I brought you this, like I promised.

MURNAU. No, don't take it out!

(*But it's too late,* **MAX** *has pulled out the script. And finally we can see why* **MURNAU** *and* **ALBIN** *are concerned. In huge block letters, the cover of the script reads: "F.W. MURNAU'S DRACULA."*)

MAX. Why not? What's wrong?

MURNAU. Moritz just received a demand from the court for any copies of the script. Yours is the only one left.

MAX. So?

MURNAU. So look at the cover, Max. It doesn't say "*Nosferatu*" does it?

MAX. It says "F.W. Murnau's *Dracula.*" Is that bad?

MURNAU. It's all Mrs. Stoker needs to prove copyright infringement. It shows we *intended* the movie to be *Dracula.*

MAX. That makes sense now.

MURNAU. So if he asks, you can't let the judge know you brought it for me. Or that you ever had it. Now give me the script so I can get rid of it. Do you have any matches?

MAX. I don't. And I'm not sure I can let you have it if the judge wants it. I can't get in trouble with the law, Freddy.

(**MAX** *clutches the script tightly.*)

MURNAU. Maxie, you owe me. Remember the make-up tests? How you begged for more and more and I gave you exactly what you wanted.

MAX. My face had to be totally disguised. I can't get typecast as a creepy monster. I need to move on to leading-man roles.

(**MURNAU** *looks* **MAX** *in the creepy face and can hardly bring himself to go along with the fantasy.*)

MURNAU. And for you and only you, I agreed. Gave you those long claws, that bald head, that pale skin...so no one would recognize your...your...*handsome* visage.

MAX. I thought it was because it would look less like how Dracula was described by Stoker.

MURNAU. No it was for *you*! I did it just for you, and now you need to do something just for me.

MAX. What?

MURNAU. Give me the script! Or tear it up and throw it out the window yourself.

MAX. Freddy, I've been so worried about being thought of by my public as a vampire. Now that the film's been seized and no one else can see it, it's almost a relief...

> (*Remember the melodramatic 'silent movie' gestures!*)

MURNAU. What are you saying, Max?

MAX. Show business is cruel, Freddy. And I'm not only thinking of myself.

MURNAU. Of course not.

MAX. If they think of you as a monster movie maker, they may never take you seriously again.

MURNAU. That is ridiculous. The film has been beautifully received.

MAX. *Today* it has. But it could fall out of favor and then...

MURNAU. Maxie, Maxie, Maxie. *This* film will make you immortal. The only thing that can taint it is if *Mrs.* Stoker wins.

> (*He draws* MAX *in close, trying to kill him with flattery. Music Begins.*)

> **[MUSIC NO. 9 – "THE NIGHT WE FILMED YOUR DEATH"]**

You can't let anything prevent the public from seeing your magnificent work. Your talent amazed me every day on the set. And there was "that scene"...you know the one I'm talking about...oh Max...

> (*He sings.*)

THE CAMERA STARTED CRANKING
THE LIGHTS WERE TURNED UP HIGH
YOU POSED BEFORE THE BACKDROP
AND FACED THE SKY –

MAX. (*creepy voice!*)
THE CANVAS SKY.

MURNAU.

> AND THE CREW JUST STOOD THERE, SPELLBOUND
> THEY WATCHED WITH BATED BREATH
> AT YOUR SKILLFUL,
> GRAND PERFORMANCE
> ON THE NIGHT WE FILMED YOUR DEATH.

MAX.

> ON THE NIGHT YOU FILMED MY DEATH!
> I HAD THOUGHT OUT MY MOTIVATION
> AND REHEARSED THE DAY BEFORE
> AND WHEN I NEEDED EXTRA TAKES
> YOU GAVE ME MORE

MURNAU.

> I GAVE YOU MORE!
> AND THE CREW JUST STOOD THERE, SPELLBOUND
> THEY WATCHED WITH BATED BREATH
> AS YOU MADE
> YOUR MARK IN HISTORY
> ON THE NIGHT WE FILMED YOUR DEATH

MAX.

> ON THE NIGHT YOU FILMED MY DEATH!

MURNAU.

> IT WAS HARD TO KILL A VAMPIRE
> IN MY MIND.
> BUT YOU GAVE ME INSPIRATION –

MAX.

> YOU'RE TOO KIND!

> *(As* **MURNAU** *continues,* **MAX** *is inspired to recreate
> his dramatic* Nosferatu *gestures – the lights flicker
> as if the movie is coming to life for a few moments.)*

MURNAU.

> YOU MADE IT LOOK SO EASY
> WHEN YOU PLAYED THE SENSE OF DOOM.
> AND I CAPTURED IT FOREVER
> AS YOUR SHADOW FILLED THE ROOM.

> FOR THE BIG CLIMATIC MOMENT
> WHEN YOU ACTED OUT YOUR HEART

I GAVE ALMOST NO DIRECTION
YOU LIVED THIS PART
YOU *WERE* THIS PART

BOTH.

AND THE CREW JUST STOOD THERE, SPELLBOUND
THEY WATCHED WITH BATED BREATH

MURNAU.

AT YOUR PHOTOGENIC GENIUS
ON THE NIGHT WE FILMED YOUR DEATH...

> (**MAX** *starts to realize he's being played.*)

ON THE NIGHT WE FILMED YOUR DEATH –

> (**MAX** *cuts short* **MURNAU***'s big final note as the music continues.*)

MAX. – Freddy, you're trying to butter me up.

MURNAU. Is it working?

MAX. No.

MURNAU. I'll film your death for real if you don't give me that script!

> (*Music dramatically ends.*)

MAX. Freddy.

MURNAU. Don't you want to be remembered as the screen's first Count Dracula?

MAX. Not if his name is Count Orlock. This is a blessing in disguise, Freddy. You'll see.

> (**MURNAU** *reaches for the script but* **MAX** *pulls it away.*)

MURNAU. Give me that damned script, you fiend!

> (**MURNAU** *dashes over the furniture and rushes toward* **MAX**, *trying to grab it.*)

MAX. I won't commit perjury! Sorry, Freddy.

> (*Remember the 'silent movie' gestures.*)

MURNAU. So the fangs finally come out!

> (**MAX** *opens the large creaking door.*)

MAX. You'll make many more films!

(He exits as **MURNAU** *rants.)*

MURNAU. Not with you, you miserable rat. Afraid of typecasting? I'll tell people you're a *real* vampire. Take the damned script! Give it to the judge! See if I care!

(Before the door closes, **ALBIN** *re-enters just in time to hear. The door creaks behind him.)*

ALBIN. I take it that didn't go well.

MURNAU. Naturally he has his own agenda. He regrets playing the vampire. He thinks he's the next Valentino! With *that face!*

ALBIN. Then there's one last chance, Freddy.

MURNAU. I scared to hear it.

ALBIN. I could ask Mrs. Stoker herself to come in and talk to you. She's been learning German. Perhaps you can reason with her.

MURNAU. *(shocked)* That wicked woman? I couldn't bear to be in the same room with her. It would be a nightmare.

ALBIN. The *real* nightmare will come true if you don't try.

(Remember the melodramatic 'silent movie' gestures!)

MURNAU. I cannot look that gorgon in the eye.

ALBIN. She holds the key to your career. Your reputation as the finest filmmaker in Germany.

*(***MURNAU*** silently contemplates.)*

MURNAU. Very well. Go get her now, before I change my mind.

*(***ALBIN*** heads for the door.)*

ALBIN. I'll send her in. Be charming, Freddy.

(With another loud creak, **ALBIN** *exits through the door.)*

MURNAU. I always am.

*(***MURNAU*** paces around the room for a moment, then turns away from the door, as if terrified of*

what may soon come through it. He mutters to himself.)

MURNAU. Don't be afraid. Don't be afraid...

[MUSIC NO. 10 – MRS. STOKER's ENTRANCE]

(The nightmarish music and lighting begin again. Finally, MRS. **FLORENCE STOKER** *[Actor Five], a haughty woman in late middle age, wearing a dark "widow's dress," comes bursting through the door like a bat out of hell. Even her long shawl suggests the wings of a vampire bat.*

MURNAU *practically jumps out of his skin as the music stops and the lights return to normal.)*

MRS. STOKER. So you're the bloodsucker.

MURNAU. You frightened me!

MRS. STOKER. I'm Mrs. Florence Stoker.

MURNAU. I know.

MRS. STOKER. And you're F.W. Murnau. The man who doesn't respect the dead.

MURNAU. My friends call me Freddy.

MRS. STOKER. And what do your victims call you?

(Remember the melodramatic 'silent movie' gestures!)

MURNAU. My *public* calls me an artist.

MRS. STOKER. My husband was an artist too. With words. *His* words.

MURNAU. I have great respect for your husband's work.

MRS. STOKER. I don't think you do or you wouldn't have stolen from him.

MURNAU. My good woman, I did not steal. It was an homage.

MRS. STOKER. That's preposterous.

(Music begins as she slowly, and carefully sings.)

[MUSIC NO. 11 – "OUT FOR BLOOD"]

> YOU'VE CAUSED A SITUATION
> THAT'S TOO BIG TO IGNORE.
> THE FACT IS I'VE BEEN WRONGED
> IT'S NEVER HAPPENED BEFORE.
> I CAN'T JUST TURN MY BACK
> BUT MUST DIVE INTO THIS MUCK
> SO YOU'RE OUT OF LUCK!
> YES, YOU'RE OUT OF LUCK!

MURNAU. Is this what your husband would have wanted?

> *(She pays no attention to him as the music intensifies and the tempo accelerates. Now she's really on a roll.)*

MRS. STOKER.

> WHEN BRAM WAS WRITING *DRACULA*
> HE DIDN'T GET PAID
> AND AFTER IT WAS PUBLISHED
> NOT A FORTUNE WAS MADE
> NOW HE'S GONE, BUT I'M PROTECTING
> WHAT HE LEFT IN HIS WILL
> HE'D BE OUT TO KILL!
> SO I'M OUT TO KILL!

MURNAU. We can add your name to the credits!

MRS. STOKER.

> I'VE NEVER BEEN A FAN OF THOSE
> WHO DON'T REVERE BOOKS
> I'VE COME TO LEARN THE CINEMA'S
> A BUISNESS FOR CROOKS
> AND I HAVE TO MAKE YOU MISERABLE –
> THE LEAST I CAN DO!
> SO I'M OUT FOR YOU!
> YES, I'M OUT FOR YOU!
>
> YOU STOLE FROM BRAM
> YOU STOLE FROM ME
> YOU'RE GONNA PAY
> YOU'RE GONNA SEE
> I'M GONNA WIN
> AND WIN WITH GLEE
> YOUR SHAMELESS COPY WILL BE MINE – FOR FREE!

MURNAU. *(pleading)* Can't we can reach an agreement?

MRS. STOKER.

> I HAVE NO OBLIGATION
> TO ACCOMMODATE FOOLS
> WHO THINK THAT THEY'RE ABOVE
> ALL OF SOCIETY'S RULES.
> I KNOW THAT YOU'D FEEL DIFFERENT
> IF THE VICTIM WERE YOU
> I KNOW WHAT YOU WOULD SAY
> AND THEN I KNOW WHAT YOU'D DO
> YOU'D VOW TO RUIN THE THIEF
> AND DRAG HIS NAME THROUGH THE MUD
> YOU'D BE OUT FOR BLOOD!
> SO I'M OUT FOR BLOOD!
>
>> (**MURNAU** *turns away; as if she's the most terrifying thing he's ever seen. But she practically chases him around the room with her black shawl flowing and flapping behind her.*)
>
> YOU MADE MISTAKES
> YOU MADE ME CRY
> YOU'RE GONNA LOSE
> AND YOU KNOW WHY.
> I'LL HAVE YOUR HEAD!
> YOUR FILM WILL DIE!
> I'LL BEAT YOU,
> DEFEAT YOU,
> TURN VAMPIRE
> AND EAT YOU!
> YOU SHOULDN'T HAVE ANY DOUBT –
> THAT MRS. STOKER IS OUT…
> FOR BLOOD!
> OUT FOR BLOOD!
> I'M OUT FOR BLOOD!
>
> *(The song ends with great melodramatic flair.)*

MURNAU. You clearly don't have your husband's gift for words, Mrs. Stoker.

MRS. STOKER. I believe that's all I have to say to you, Mr. Murnau.

(She turns toward the door, he blocks her.)

MURNAU. Wait. Don't go.

(She stops.)

Didn't you notice all the changes we made? It's not *exactly* your husband's story.

MRS. STOKER. I haven't seen it.

MURNAU. Then we should arrange it. You should at least see how well directed it is.

MRS. STOKER. I have no intention of *ever* seeing it.

MURNAU. You don't want to experience the greatest horror film in the history of German cinema?

MRS. STOKER. I thought that distinction belonged to *The Cabinet of Dr. Caligari.*

MURNAU. Yesterday's news! I don't understand. If you didn't see it, how did you even find out about it? It was never referred to in the press as *Dracula.*

MRS. STOKER. I received an anonymous letter along with a program from the Berlin premiere.

MURNAU. Anonymous letter? Sounds like something out of one of my movies.

MRS. STOKER. Speaking of your movies, I've been told of your wonderful *Dr. Jekyll & Mr. Hyde.*

MURNAU. *(flattered)* Well, it wasn't *called* that, but yes, very successful. A fascinating actor named Bela Lugosi was brilliant in a small role. I even considered him for *Drac... Nosferatu,* but he didn't seem like the vampire type.

MRS. STOKER. Mr. Lugosi is irrelevant to *Dracula.* But apparently you also neglected to get the rights from the Robert Louis Stevenson estate.

MURNAU. Details! And *they* never dared sue!

MRS. STOKER. If you're interested in *Dorian Gray,* Mr. Murnau, I once dated Oscar Wilde –

MURNAU. *(pointedly sarcastic)* He must have been quite a catch for you.

(She coldly glares at him and starts to leave.)

(**MURNAU** *runs in front of the door.*)

MURNAU. Mrs. Stoker, how can I appease you?

MRS. STOKER. By conceding.

MURNAU. *Nosferatu* is *my* creation, and what few things it has in common with *Dracula* are a mere coincidence.

MRS. STOKER. Let me level with you, sir. My husband's copyright belongs to *me* now and I'm negotiating with a producer who wants to put *Dracula* on Broadway and then bring it to Hollywood. I can't let there be an *illegal* competing version.

(**MURNAU** *gasps in melodramatic horror, as if he can't believe what he's just heard.*)

MURNAU. Ah ha! So much for art. It's all about *business.*

(*He turns away in disgust as her music begins again.*)

[*MUSIC NO. 12 – "OUT FOR BLOOD" – TAG*]

MRS. STOKER. I'm leaving now, Mr. Murnau. It's in the hands of the judge. And I'm very confident about the outcome.

(*Music intensifies. She sings.*)

YOU SHOULDN'T HAVE ANY DOUBT –
THAT MRS. STOKER IS OUT...
FOR BLOOD!
OUT FOR BLOOD, OUT FOR BLOOD,
I'M OUT FOR BLOOD!

(*She heads for the door. He calls after her.*)

MURNAU. So am I!

(*In a flourish, she exits with a door slam. Music ends.*

MURNAU *nervously mops his brow with a handkerchief.*)

Damn it, damn it, damn it!

(The door begins to creak open again. MURNAU *panics, but relaxes as* ALBIN *enters.)*

ALBIN. Freddy...

MURNAU. It didn't work. I couldn't convince her.

ALBIN. What do you mean?

MURNAU. She wouldn't listen to reason.

ALBIN. Freddy, she refused to see you. She's been sitting in the courtroom, reading.

[MUSIC NO. 13 – STING CUES (SECOND SET)]

(The blood drains from MURNAU*'s face. Underscore "sting.")*

MURNAU. What? But she was just in here.

(Underscore bigger "sting.")

ALBIN. *(in a creepy tone)* Impossible. You must have imagined it.

(Underscore even bigger "sting.")

MURNAU. *(panicked)* Oh dear lord, I'm hallucinating... I thought she was here... I... I...talked to her. Albin... you've got to help me – I'm going crazy!

ALBIN. *(laughing)* Don't lose your head, Freddy. I was just kidding. I escorted her to the door myself.

(Remember the 'silent movie' gestures!)

MURNAU. Damn you, man! Are you trying to put me in a mental ward? You scared me to death.

ALBIN. You needed a good scare.

MURNAU. I learned how she found out about the film. An anonymous letter! And I'll bet my life it was from Max! That traitor!

ALBIN. He really is a monster.

MURNAU. Worse than that, he's...an artist!

[MUSIC NO. 14 – SILENT MOVIE UNDERSCORE – MORITZ RE-ENTERS]

(The door creaks open, causing them both to jump. Melancholy underscore begins as **MORITZ** *slowly walks in. He is shaking and afraid to talk.)*

ALBIN. Don't just stand there shaking, Moritz. What is it?

MORITZ. *(hardly getting the words out)* The judge...he...he took one look at Herr Schreck's screenplay with the title *Dracula* and ruled against us.

(He braces himself to be screamed at. But **MURNAU** *and* **ALBIN** *just stay silent for a bit.)*

ALBIN. How much do we have to pay now?

MORITZ. Nothing.

MURNAU. Nothing? What do you mean nothing?

MORITZ. The judge believed your financial disclosures. He knows there isn't any money to be paid.

MURNAU. So we can exhibit the movie again...to earn money to pay the Stoker estate?

MORITZ. Not exactly.

MURNAU. Then what exactly?

MORITZ. The judge has ordered every print of *Nosferatu* to be...to be...to be...

ALBIN. Spit it out, man!

MORITZ. To be destroyed. Including the negative.

(Underscore dramatically ends. **MURNAU** *and* **ALBIN** *are stunned.)*

MURNAU. It really *is* a nightmare come true. Or is *this* the nightmare and I'm still asleep?

ALBIN. Why would the judge create such a harsh punishment?

MORITZ. It's what Frau Stoker asked for.

(Remember the 'silent movie' gestures!)

MURNAU. I'm ruined.

ALBIN. Freddy...

MURNAU. *(inconsolable)* My work...destroyed. Gone forever like a vanquished vampire. Leaving me a mere mortal without a soul...

ALBIN. Moritz, will you please get out of here?

MORITZ. Yes, sir.

> (**MORITZ** *hurriedly exits, barely managing the door.* **ALBIN** *moves to console the devastated* **MURNAU**.)

ALBIN. Freddy. It may not be gone forever.

MURNAU. What do you mean? With a judgment like that, we can never...

ALBIN. Never allow it to be shown in Germany. Or nearby.

MURNAU. So?

ALBIN. I had an extra print struck. I paid for it myself, right after we were served the legal papers.

MURNAU. *(stunned)* That must have cost you a fortune. Where is it?

ALBIN. In America.

MURNAU. America?

ALBIN. I sent it to an old friend who's a film collector in Hollywood.

MURNAU. Thank you, Albin. But if Mrs. Stoker gets wind of it...

ALBIN. Mrs. Stoker won't live forever. And as long as it's kept underground for a while, it will have the chance to resurface someday. I'll make sure of it.

MURNAU. Hollywood is where I belong too. I'm going to be a laughing stock in Germany.

ALBIN. But this is your home.

MURNAU. My home is where my masterpiece is.

ALBIN. I suppose I could make a few calls for you. Do you know what you'd want to film?

MURNAU. I had an idea, but there's already some studio out there making a movie out of Leroux's *Phantom of the Opera*.

ALBIN. An *opera* with no sound?

MURNAU. That's why I belong in Hollywood. They're so audacious! And far more forgiving of artists.

ALBIN. You mean of thieves?

(Remember the 'silent movie' gestures!)

MURNAU. Albin!

ALBIN. I'm just kidding.

MURNAU. Do you think they'll recognize me as the creator of the first cinematic… *Dracula*?

ALBIN. I hope so, Freddy.

MURNAU. What if your friend doesn't properly care for the film and it disintegrates? Will it be remembered at all? Will I?

ALBIN. Have faith, man. I'll go see what the judge's order looks like on paper.

(He moves to leave.)

MURNAU. Thank you for not saying it.

ALBIN. For not saying what?

MURNAU. That it was all my fault. That I stole *Dracula* outright and I deserve what's happened

ALBIN. *(warmly)* If I really wanted to, I could have stopped you. But I believed in it too.

> *(**ALBIN** exits. The door creaks behind him. **MURNAU** is totally defeated. Music begins as the lights slowly begin to darken behind him until he is left standing in a pool of light, casting an enormous shadow. Scenery can begin to change in darkness.)*
>
> *[MUSIC NO. 15 – "SACRIFICE" – ACT ONE FINALE]*
>
> *(He sings.)*

MURNAU.

> I WON'T SACRIFICE MY VISION
> NO MATTER IF IT'S BORROWED –
> STILL I NEVER
> CROSSED THE LINE.
> THOUGH NOW MY FILM
> IS A TARGET FOR DERISION,

I'LL STILL DEFEND MY VAMPIRE –
HE'LL BE FINE...
EVEN IF THE VAMPIRE'S
NOT QUITE MINE.

> (**MURNAU** *contemplates for a moment, then gets his bravado back and speaks to the heavens.*)

I knew I should have filmed *Frankenstein* instead. That book's over a hundred years old! And I know just how I would have done it...a real F.W. Murnau spectacle... thunder...lightning... Oh, if only pictures had sound!

> (*The music crescendos as the lights focus on* **MURNAU***'s shadowy face. Blackout.*)

[MUSIC NO. 16 – TRANSITION TO ACT TWO]

> (*Music sneaks back in as we suddenly hear the deafeningly loud crash of thunder and lightning, which leads us to...*)

ACT TWO
"I'VE CREATED A MONSTER"

Scene One: Pre-Production
Hollywood, 1931.
The Make-Up Room At Universal Studios

(A single window is revealed high on a wall. A menacing thunderstorm is raging outside of it. Music changes tone.)

[MUSIC NO. 17 – "CREATING A MONSTER" – ACT TWO OPENING]

(As the storm continues, the lights slowly come up on the make-up room at Universal Studios in Hollywood. But it's not just any make-up room, it looks like a mad scientist's laboratory. Decorating the room are stone walls, tables and shelves housing an array of spooky-looking make-up jars, chemicals, powders, brushes, tools, sponges, etc. Everything is in stark black & white or gray-scale, including the costumes.

In the center of the room is a reclining make-up chair [like a barber's chair] that almost looks like a medieval torture device.

JACK PIERCE *[Actor Two], a man in his late 30s, wearing small, round spectacles and a white barber's smock that resembles a lab-coat, stands in the middle of the room. He is the head of the make-up department but seems more like a genial mad-scientist. He is giddy with excitement as he mixes a grayish concoction in a large beaker.*

A loud bolt of lightning outside the window almost causes him to almost drop the beaker. **PIERCE** *talks to himself as he gazes at the mixture.)*

PIERCE. Oh careful, careful. I'd hate to lose this beautiful consistency.

(As the storm rages around him, he slowly sings.)

WHEN I'M CREATING A MONSTER,
IT TAKES PRACTICE AND PATIENCE
EACH DAY.
I MUST ASSEMBLE THE PARTS
AND FORGET THE FALSE STARTS
AND KEEP IT ALL IN DISTINCT SHADES OF GREY...

(As the music continues, he resumes mixing by adding powders to alter the color. He cackles with enjoyment as he holds it up to get a closer look.)

Ah, that's perfect...*perfect!*

(VERA WEST [Actor Five], a wisecracking gal in her late 30s and head of the costume department, enters with a few garment bags and a newspaper. The music eventually subsides.)

VERA. Good morning, Jack. I brought three sample costume choices for the tests today.

(A lightning flash. VERA jumps.)

Jeez, will this storm ever end!?

(PIERCE looks out the window.)

PIERCE. Thank you, Vera. Is it really still morning? It's pitch black out there.

VERA. It looks so scary. I never thought I'd be glad Universal gave me a wardrobe room with no windows.

(She puts the garment bags on a table, and opens the newspaper.)

I also wanted to show you this in the paper. Who is F.W. Murnau?

PIERCE. Never heard of him. Why?

VERA. He was in the business. Came over from Germany. A director. Says he worked mostly in "silents."

PIERCE. Oh. What about him?

VERA. He's dead. Died in a car crash.

PIERCE. That's a shame. A real horror.

(She points to a passage in the paper.)

VERA. There's a quote from Lugosi. Apparently Murnau once worked with him.

PIERCE. *(disgusted)* Lugosi! It's bad enough *we* have to work with him again. I may have to see that man today but don't make me *read* about him too.

VERA. Sorry.

(She folds up the newspaper as **CARL LAEMMLE** *[Actor Four], the head of Universal Studios, enters. He is a middle-aged, typical Hollywood-type.)*

CARL. Excuse me, Jack, Vera.

(He looks around at the surroundings.)

Holy smoke! What kind of set-up do you have here, Jack? All of this is *make-up?*

VERA. Haven't you ever come down here, Carl?

CARL. No, I only sign the checks to keep the electricity on.

(He picks up an odd looking container of something unidentifiable.)

PIERCE. Don't touch that!

*(**CARL** quickly puts it back.)*

CARL. I have some very important production news for *Frankenstein.*

VERA. What is it?

PIERCE. Good news I hope.

CARL. We just fired Bela Lugosi.

VERA. What?

PIERCE. That's the best news I've ever heard in my life. What happened?

CARL. You know how insulted he felt being cast as the monster instead of the doctor.

PIERCE. Mmm hmm.

CARL. He gave me an ultimatum to change my mind, or said he'd quit, along with his director of choice. So they're both off of *Frankenstein* – I gave them a "B" picture to fulfill their contracts.

VERA. The director too? But we're about to start.

CARL. Don't worry, we're staying right on schedule. I hired a swell guy from England. He's upstairs signing his contract right now. James Whale.

PIERCE. Never heard of him.

VERA. But who's playing the monster?

CARL. A fine actor named Boris Karloff.

PIERCE. Boris who?

CARL. Karloff.

PIERCE. I've never heard of him either.

VERA. Jack, have you ever heard of *anyone?*

PIERCE. What's he been in?

CARL. Small roles here and there. But he's got the right look. And he's very, very cheap.

PIERCE. I thought we had a good budget for this.

CARL. We do. But I always like to save a little. And if he works out, we'll have created a new star – with an exclusive contract. He's coming in to meet you any moment.

PIERCE. As long as he has a pliable face.

CARL. He's also from England.

PIERCE. Aren't there any suitable Americans anymore?

> (**BORIS KARLOFF** [Actor Three], *a British actor in his early 40s with an unmistakable voice, enters behind them.*)

KARLOFF. I've spent most of my life in America if that's important.

> (**PIERCE**, **VERA** *and* **CARL** *turn to see him.*)

CARL. There you are, Boris!

(He makes introductions.)

CARL. Jack Pierce – head of make-up; Vera West – wardrobe mistress, this is Mr. Boris Karloff.

KARLOFF. How do you do?

PIERCE. Hi. I'm the man who's going to turn you into a monster, Boris.

KARLOFF. Oh, I know all about you, Mr. Pierce. I'm a great admirer of your work.

PIERCE. Thanks. It's so refreshing to have an actor compliment someone other than himself.

(KARLOFF laughs.)

CARL. Boris, Jack, I'll leave you two to work on the make-up!

PIERCE. Excellent.

CARL. Vera, let's go down to wardrobe. I need to you to walk me through the costumes.

VERA. Gee, I sure hope this new director isn't gonna change anything.

CARL. Jack, we'll be ready to see the make-up tests this afternoon.

PIERCE. Oh it'll take longer than that. Early evening.

CARL. *Very* early evening.

(CARL and VERA exit.)

PIERCE. Won't you sit down in my chair, Boris?

(Thunder and lightning as KARLOFF sits in the make-up chair. PIERCE pulls a lever that forcefully reclines him almost all the way backward, to KARLOFF's surprise. [If such a chair is not practical, PIERCE can just forcefully push him into the seat with gleeful zeal.] KARLOFF tries to get comfortable and looks around the unusual room.)

KARLOFF. I've never been in a make-up room like this, Mr. Pierce.

(PIERCE adjusts the angle to upright KARLOFF.)

PIERCE. Thank you! And call me Jack.

KARLOFF. Jack.

PIERCE. Now let me at that face!

> *(He excitedly holds **KARLOFF**'s face in his hands.)*

Will you let me try *anything*, Boris?

KARLOFF. You're the artist.

PIERCE. I'm going to like you! Now relax. First I'm going to apply a little cucumber juice so we have a good foundation to start with.

> *(**PIERCE**, gets a bottle of a clear liquid and starts rubbing all over his face. **KARLOFF** jumps.)*

KARLOFF. That's cold!

> *(**PIERCE** pays no attention to him.)*

PIERCE. This is going to be so much fun now that I don't have to deal with Lugosi! You wouldn't believe the trouble I had with him on *Dracula*. I designed something glorious for his face. A hairpiece, distinctive brows, wrinkled eye-lids, a devilish false mustache. But he insisted on doing his own make-up "just like on the *stage!*" Can you imagine? In the movie he looked like... like a regular person!

> *(**KARLOFF** finds it difficult to comment with his face in **PIERCE**'s hands.)*

KARLOFF. *(muffled)* Outrageous!

> *(**PIERCE** continues to happily rub the cold liquid all over **KARLOFF**'s face, pulling his head to and fro.)*

PIERCE. Who wants a vampire to look like a regular person? That's not horror. I'd resigned myself to a simple approach for *Frankenstein*. But with you, Boris, I can go all out. You're clearly a natural monster!

KARLOFF. Thank you.

PIERCE. Now let me have a closer look.

> *(Music begins, punctuated by the thunder and lightning.)*

[MUSIC NO. 18 – "CREATING A MONSTER"]

*(He peers closely at **KARLOFF**.)*

PIERCE. Boris, I don't like your pallor. I'm going to have to change it!

KARLOFF. Change it into what?

PIERCE. I haven't decided yet! Just keep holding still!

*(Lightning strikes. **PIERCE** sings as he closely inspects **KARLOFF**'s face.)*

MY SECRET WAY
TO CHANGE THE SKIN
INVOLVES SCUPLTING AND SHAPING AND SHADING
I'VE SEEN COLLEAGUES TRY TO DO THIS –
WELL, AT LEAST, BEGIN
BUT THEY CAN'T STOP THE MAKE-UP FROM FADING.
ACTORS CALL ME A SADIST
WHILE IN MY CHAIR
'CAUSE IT'S HARD TO ENDURE ALL THE PAINTING
THEY GET MAD AS HELL
IF I BURN THEIR HAIR
BUT THE RESULTS ARE WORTH
ALL OF THE FAINTING

*(**KARLOFF**'s eyes widen with semi-fear as **PIERCE** begins to dry off his skin with a towel.)*

WHEN I'M CREATING A MONSTER
I MUST GIVE THE MONSTER RESPECT
IT WILL BE STALE AND LOOK OLD
IF I DON'T BREAK THE MOLD
AND GIVE 'EM SOMETHING THAT THEY WON'T EXPECT!

I DON'T FORGET
WHEN CREATING A MONSTER
THAT THE MONSTER'S THE HERO TO ME!
IT'S MEANT TO BE FRIGHT'NING
BUT JUST LIKE THE LIGHTNING
INSPIRATION WILL STRIKE
TO SET A NEW MONSTER FREE!

*(**KARLOFF** cautiously joins in the song.)*

KARLOFF.

> IT'S MEANT TO BE FRIGHT'NING
> BUT JUST LIKE THE LIGHTNING
> THERE'S A MONSTER THAT YOU SOON WILL SET FREE!

> *(**KARLOFF** adjusts his posture.)*

How exactly will you start? You're not going to shave anything off, are you?

PIERCE.

> I'M GLAD YOU'VE ASKED
> OF HOW I WORK
> I LIKE TO EXPERIMENT ON FACES
> TURN THE BRIGHTEST SMILE
> INTO AN EVIL SMIRK
> AND PUT SCARS
> IN THE LOGICAL PLACES!

> *(He gets out a box of hair-pieces and starts testing them out on **KARLOFF**'s head.)*

> WHEN I'M CREATING A MONSTER
> I MUST GIVE THE MONSTER RESPECT
> IT WILL BE STALE AND LOOK OLD
> IF I DON'T BREAK THE MOLD
> AND GIVE 'EM SOMETHING THAT I CAN PERFECT.

> I DON'T FORGET
> WHEN CREATING A MONSTER
> THAT IT HAS TO STAND OUT FROM THE CROWD!
> IT'S GREASEPAINT, BUT SO MUCH MORE
> FINDING THE INNER CORE!
> IT'S POWDER AND COLOR AND WIG
> THAT MAKE A MAKE-UP MAN PROUD –

KARLOFF.

> GREASEPAINT, BUT SO MUCH MORE
> FINDING THE INNER CORE
> IT ALL MAKES A MAKE-UP MAN PROUD!

> *(The music continues as **PIERCE** excitedly reaches for a large jar of make-up.)*

PIERCE. Let's try some of this!

KARLOFF. It's *green*.

PIERCE. Yes! It should look deathly in black & white. Oh if only this film was in color! I love color! Let's test it out on your hands.

> *(He starts dabbing a bit of the green make-up [which in reality is in gray-scale, like the rest of the set] onto* KARLOFF's *hands.)*

Perfect! Boris...you will be my *greatest creation*!

> **(PIERCE** *laughs maniacally in delight.)*

KARLOFF. My word, you're a bit like Dr. Frankenstein himself!

PIERCE. Sometimes I get carried away!

> **(PIERCE** *laughs again, and tightly ties a dark protective cloth around* KARLOFF's *neck.* KARLOFF *isn't sure if he should be afraid or not.)*

SAY GOODBYE
TO STYLES THAT ARE OUT OF DATE
SAY GOODBYE
TO BLAND OR OVERDONE
SAY GOODBYE
TO THE WAY HE'S WRITTEN ON THE PAGE
SAY HELLO
TO A CREATURE
THAT WILL
MAKE THEM
SCREAM AND RUN!

NOW LET ME TRY
FOR SOMETHING FRESH
YOU CAN WATCH IF YOU DON'T TOUCH MY BRUSHES
WHILE I MIX A BATCH OF
DECAYING FLESH
SO SIT BACK AS INVENTIVENESS GUSHES

> **(KARLOFF** *is finally comfortable enough to practically dance along in the chair.)*

PIERCE.

>WHEN I'M CREATING A MONSTER
>I MUST GIVE THE MONSTER RESPECT
>IT WILL BE STALE AND LOOK OLD
>IF I DON'T BREAK THE MOLD
>AND GIVE 'EM MORE THAN A SPECIAL EFFECT!

>I DON'T FORGET
>WHEN CREATING A MONSTER
>THAT THE MONSTER IS ONLY A MAN!
>BUT ONCE I VENEER YOU
>THE PUBLIC WILL FEAR YOU
>I'LL BRING THE MONSTER TO LIFE
>LIKE NO ONE ELSE CAN!

KARLOFF.

>ONCE YOU VENEER ME
>THE PUBLIC WILL FEAR ME
>BRING THE MONSTER TO LIFE
>LIKE NO ONE ELSE CAN!

PIERCE.

>LIKE NO ONE ELSE CAN!

KARLOFF.

>LIKE NO ONE ELSE CAN!

PIERCE.

>NO ONE ELSE CAN!

>>*(Music crescendos as* **PIERCE** *grabs* **KARLOFF**'s *face.)*

KARLOFF. Could you at least warm your hands please, Jack!?

>>*(With a thunderous, majestic chord, the music ends.*

>>**PIERCE** *laughs manically as* **JAMES WHALE** *[Actor One], a calm, well-mannered, nicely dressed man in his early 40s, enters.)*

WHALE. Pardon me, is this the make-up room?

PIERCE. Yes, may I help you?

WHALE. *(grandly)* I am James Whale.

PIERCE. *(unimpressed)* Oh yes, the new director. I'm Jack Pierce. *Head* of the Make-up department, and this is Boris Karloff – your star.

KARLOFF. My word, Jack, the monster isn't the *star*. Hello, Mr. Whale.

>(**WHALE** *shakes hands with both of them.*)

WHALE. It's a pleasure to meet you both. I'm looking forward to getting started. I've just gotten the script and I'm making some changes. Improvements I'm sure.

PIERCE. What kind of improvements?

WHALE. I cut all of the monster's lines.

KARLOFF. You did what?

PIERCE. Are we going back to the silent days?

WHALE. Mrs. Shelley should have done it my way. But now that her monster is in the public domain, I think he'll be far more frightening if he doesn't speak.

KARLOFF. Frightening all right.

WHALE. Don't worry Mr. Karloff. If you listen to me, I'll make you famous.

KARLOFF. That sounds marvelous.

>(**PIERCE** *moves toward* **KARLOFF**'s *face with a brush.*)

PIERCE. Hold still please, Boris.

>(**WHALE** *moves in front of* **PIERCE** *to take control of* **KARLOFF**.*)

WHALE. It's all in the approach, Mr. Karloff… and I promise that I know just what to do.

>(*Music begins.* **PIERCE** *moves to take control again.*)

>[*MUSIC NO. 19 – REPRISE – "CREATING A MONSTER [QUARTET]"*]

PIERCE. Mr. Whale, please…

(PIERCE preps KARLOFF's face as WHALE sings to him, constantly getting in PIERCE's way.)

WHALE.

WHEN I'M CREATING A MONSTER
IT TAKES FOCUS AND NUANCE AND SKILL
I'LL HAVE YOU ACT WITH YOUR EYES
SINCE WE MUST SYMPATHIZE
EVEN WHEN YOU MOVE IN FOR THE KILL.

AND I'LL MAKE SURE,
WHEN CREATING A MONSTER –
WHO CAN'T TALK AND HAS NO LINES TO SAY,
THAT IF YOU DON'T GET IN FIGHTS
AND TRUST MY LENS AND MY LIGHTS,
WE'LL MAKE A CLASSIC OF THIS GENRE
AS I MOLD YOU LIKE CLAY!

(Music continues. VERA enters with a tape measure around her neck.)

VERA. I need to borrow Mr. Karloff for a few minutes to get his measurements.

(She notices WHALE.)

Oh hello.

WHALE. I'm James Whale. And you must be Vera West.

(WHALE kisses her hand. It excites her.)

VERA. Yes, I must be.

WHALE. I was just telling Mr. Karloff that even with no lines, Frankenstein's monster will be a wonderful role. And the costumes will play a very significant part in that too.

VERA. Oh, my…yes. Yes I think so. I *hope* so…

(She sings to KARLOFF.)

WHEN I'M CREATING A MONSTER
IT TAKES WARDROBE AND PADDING AND SHOES
AND THEY MUST ALL BE DEVISED
TO MAKE YOU LOOK OVERSIZED
I'VE BEEN SEARCHING FOR CLOTHES I CAN USE

THERE ARE NO RULES
FOR CREATING A MONSTER
I CAN'T LOOK TO THE SCREENPLAY FOR CLUES
WE'LL TRY ON THE SUIT
AND DECIDE ON WHICH BOOT
AND PUT IT ALL ON WITH BOLTS AND WITH SCREWS.

*(**WHALE** nudges **VERA** out of the way.)*

KARLOFF.

I'LL TRY ON THE SUIT
AND BE BRUTAL, YET MUTE
AND QUITE THE MONSTER, IF I FOLLOW YOUR CUES.

WHALE. That's the idea, my good man!

*(**PIERCE** takes control of **KARLOFF** again.)*

PIERCE.

SAY GOODBYE
TO UNINSPIRED MAKE-UP NOW!

VERA.

SAY GOODBYE
TO THE COSTUMES THAT THEY'VE SEEN

WHALE.

SAY GOODBYE
TO THOSE BORING OLD DIRECTORS NOW!

WHALE, PIERCE & VERA.

SAY HELLO
TO A CREATURE
THAT WILL
JUMP RIGHT OFF THE SCREEN!

*(**WHALE** leads **KARLOFF** out of the chair and directs him to do a few "monster walks" with arms outstretched, lumbering gait, pretending to strangle **VERA**, etc. **PIERCE** keeps cutting in with his make-up brush. It's clearly a contest between **PIERCE** and **WHALE** for **KARLOFF**'s attention. Even **VERA** tries to jump in with her tape-measure, but to no avail. They ad-lib, "Like this, Boris!" "Come back, Boris!" etc. Finally **PIERCE** wins and gets **KARLOFF** back in the chair.)*

PIERCE.

A BOLD APPROACH IS ALL IT TAKES –

VERA.

BECAUSE HORROR IS SO UNIVERSAL!

WHALE.

WE CAN RAISE THE DEAD!

WE CAN RAISE THE STAKES!

KARLOFF.

THOUGH WE HARDLY HAVE TIME FOR REHEARSAL!

WHALE, PIERCE & VERA.

SO WHEN WE START FILMING THE MONSTER

AND YOU ASK WHAT THE MONSTER WOULD DO

JUST REMEMBER YOUR TRAINING

AND BE ENTERTAINING

AND WE'LL MAKE A SCARY MONSTER –

OUT OF A NICE GUY LIKE YOU!

KARLOFF.

REMEMBER MY TRAINING

AND BE ENTERTAINING –

KARLOFF, WHALE, PIERCE & WEST.

AND WE ALL WILL MAKE A MONSTER –

KARLOFF.

– MONSTER!

WHALE, PIERCE & WEST.

MONSTER – OUT OF YOU!

KARLOFF.

OUT OF ME!

WHALE, PIERCE & WEST.

OUT OF YOU!

KARLOFF.

OUT OF ME!

KARLOFF, WHALE, PIERCE & WEST.

AND WE'LL ALL GET

A MONSTER RAVE REVIEW!

*(Music ends as they all gather around **KARLOFF**.)*

WHALE. Well, we're certainly off to a delightful start.

VERA. It's going to be exciting to work with you, Mr. Whale.

WHALE. Thank you, dear. I'll talk about the costumes with you later. For now, Mr. Pierce, can we discuss the make-up?

PIERCE. I can tell *you* what it's going to look like, yes.

VERA. Mr. Karloff, please come with me and I'll get those measurements.

KARLOFF. All right, should I come back here when we're finished, Jack?

PIERCE. Yes.

WHALE. *No.* I'll see you down on the soundstage first. Then you can come back here.

KARLOFF. I'll see you both later then.

> (**KARLOFF** *unties the cloth from around his neck and exits with* **VERA**. **PIERCE** *tinkers with his jars.*)

WHALE. You'll have to excuse me, Mr. Pierce. I'm just not myself today.

PIERCE. What's the matter?

WHALE. I'm devastated over the loss of a brother filmmaker. F.W. Murnau.

PIERCE. I heard about that. Did you know him well?

WHALE. I never met him.

PIERCE. Then why are you devastated?

WHALE. There's but for the grace of God, dear man. There but for the grace. And I greatly admired his work.

PIERCE. What films did he make?

WHALE. Well for one, the father of all horror films, *Nosferatu.*

PIERCE. I've never heard of it.

WHALE. A masterpiece.

PIERCE. What's the best thing about it?

WHALE. I never saw it.

PIERCE. Oh?

WHALE. Almost no one has. It's a long, horrifying story. But I have seen stills and posters.

PIERCE. That's nice. Now, I suppose I should tell you what the monster will look like...

> *(Lightning strikes like a light bulb over* **WHALE***'s head.)*

WHALE. The monster. Of course. A wonderful idea! As a tribute from one masterful director to another, we'll turn our Frankenstein's monster into an homage to Murnau's vampire.

PIERCE. Steal someone else's work!?

WHALE. Borrow. And no one will really even know. He's bald, with pale white skin. Big eyes. Pointed chin. Long fingernails.

PIERCE. Sounds like a perfect *vampire.* But we're making a movie about a re-animated corpse, brought back to life with electricity.

WHALE. Oh, what difference does it make? A monster's a monster.

> *(***PIERCE*** practically chokes.)*

PIERCE. No! No! No! This is Lugosi all over again. You'll ruin my vision. *I'm* in charge of the monster's look.

WHALE. I'm the *director.* I'm in charge of the whole film.

PIERCE. Do you plan to mix the face-paint yourself? Because you'll have to.

WHALE. My dear man...

PIERCE. Believe me, you will love what I have planned. For Lugosi it would have been simple. But for Karloff, I see...scars...color...

WHALE. No scars. No color.

PIERCE. *(pointedly)* Maybe you'd like a flattened skull?

WHALE. I want bald, pale, pointed chin. And I want to see a test of it *today.* And if that's a problem for you, then take it up with Mr. Laemmle. He gave me carte blanche on this picture.

*(Thunder booms. **PIERCE** thinks and finally relents.)*

PIERCE. Well then. I suppose I need to pull a bald cap.

WHALE. Thank you. I'll see you on the set.

(He exits. Thunder and lightning continue to rage.)

PIERCE. Yes, Mr. Whale I'll give you what you want. *Today.* But when we start shooting, Dr. Frankenstein's monster will be bald and pale over *my dead body*!!!

*(More lightning strikes as **PIERCE** laughs manically. Blackout.)*

[MUSIC NO. 20 – TRANSITION TO ACT TWO SCENE TWO]

Scene Two: In Production
Several Days Later

*(The lights restore on the empty make-up room. The storm still rages outside the window. **WHALE**, uncharacteristically angry and animated, comes barging in, trailed by **CARL**.)*

WHALE. Where is he!? I'm going to murder him!

CARL. Please stay calm, James.

WHALE. Calm? You want me to be calm? I've got an entire cast and crew on that soundstage waiting for me to call action, and I can't because of Jack Pierce and his damned monster make-up!

CARL. Let me worry about the cast and crew.

WHALE. I told him I wanted it *my* way…and he *switched* it!

> *(**PIERCE** emerges from a hidden area, cleaning his make-up brushes.)*

PIERCE. Are you looking for me?

WHALE. Let me at him!

> *(**CARL** stops **WHALE** from lunging at **PIERCE**, who just stands amused.)*

CARL. Now James, there's no need for *that.* Jack, what do you have to say for yourself?

WHALE. Yes, let's hear your *last words.*

PIERCE. *My* design for the monster is spectacular. *His* idea was a spur of the moment lark that hit him after that silent movie director died.

WHALE. Yours was a lark too. You had a different plan for Lugosi.

PIERCE. Don't mention that man's name!

> *(Thunder and lightning intensifies. Music begins.)*

> [MUSIC NO. 21 – "I WANT IT MY WAY"]

WHALE. For the love of God, why is there always such bad weather in Hollywood?

CARL. Let's everyone take a breath and talk this out.

WHALE. I'll do no such thing. He has to re-do the make-up.
Now.

PIERCE. And if I refuse?

WHALE. *(angrily sings)*
IF YOU WANT TO STAY
IN THIS BUISNESS, MAN
YOU NEED TO LEARN TO LISTEN TO ME
I'M THE DIRECTOR, I HAVE MY OWN PLAN
AND YOU WILL SIMPLY HAVE TO AGREE

> *(PIERCE turns away, but WHALE gets right in his face.)*

AND IF YOU THINK
THAT I'M BEING TOO TOUGH
THEN I'LL ONLY GET THAT MUCH TOUGHER
I'M THE DIRECTOR, I'VE HAD QUITE ENOUGH
SO IT'S YOUR TURN NOW TO SUFFER
I WANT IT MY WAY!
I WANT IT MY WAY!
I WANT IT MY WAY!

PIERCE. Carl, I won't listen to this madness. I'm in charge
of make-up, aren't I?

> *(Before CARL can answer, WHALE continues.)*

WHALE.
FILMS CAN'T BE COLLABORATIONS
SOMEONE MUST HAVE CONTROL
AND I DON'T BELIEVE IN NEGOTIATIONS
WE ALL MUST WORK TO ACHIEVE *MY* GOAL!

> *(WHALE grabs a towel and thrusts it at PIERCE.)*

SO YOU'D BETTER WIPE
ALL THAT UGLY GREEN
OFF HIS FACE – I DID NOT APPROVE IT
HOW YOU SQUARED HIS HEAD,
I COULD NOT HAVE FORESEEN
YOU'RE REQUIRED TO REMOVE IT!
I WANT IT MY WAY!
I WANT IT MY WAY!
I WANT IT MY WAY!

PIERCE. You are a maniac.

> (**WHALE** *pays no attention to* **PIERCE**.)

WHALE.
>
> THOSE THINGS ON HIS NECK
> WHATEVER THEY ARE
> HAVE TO GO, YOU CAN JUST UNGLUE THEM!
> AND THE JET BLACK HAIR
> AND THAT GREAT BIG SCAR
> YOU CAN DO THE SAME THING TO THEM
> I WANT IT MY WAY!

> > (**WHALE** *picks up a bald cap and throws it at* **PIERCE**.)

PIERCE. *My* way is better.

WHALE.
>
> FILMS CAN'T BE COLLABORATIONS
> I DON'T NEED INPUT AT ALL
> I LIKE MY WORK TO BE FREE OF FRUSTRATIONS
> AND RIGHT NOW I CAN'T BELIEVE YOUR GALL!
>
> YOU LIED TO MY CAST
> DISRUPTED MY SET
> RUINED MY AGENDA
> AND I'LL NEVER FORGET!
> I'D LOVE TO KILL YOU –
> IF I JUST HAD A KNIFE
> AND THERE'S NO DOCTOR WHO CAN
> BRING YOU BACK TO LIFE!

> > (**PIERCE** *laughs as* **WHALE**'s *tantrum proceeds.*)

> SO BORIS'LL REPORT
> TO THIS GODFORSAKEN ROOM –
> YOU CAN SOAK HIM IN DETERGENT
> THEN MAKE HIM LOOK RIGHT,
> SO THAT I CAN RESUME
> THERE'S A SCHEDULE, SO IT'S URGENT
> I WANT IT MY WAY!
> I WANT IT MY WAY!
> I WANT IT MY WAY!

PIERCE. *(mocking him)* What was that again?

> *(Music relaxes.)*

WHALE.

> YOUR ATTITUDE SIR,
> HAS BEGUN TO WEAR THIN
> YOU ARE CLEARLY TOO AMBITIOUS
> AND I CAN'T STAND TO LOOK
> AT YOUR SMUG LITTLE GRIN
> ARE YOU REALLY SO MALICIOUS?

PIERCE. Let the *real* artists do their work.

> **(WHALE** *has to suppress his every urge to sock* **PIERCE** *in the gut.)*

WHALE.

> NOW I THINK I'VE BEEN CLEAR
> AND EXTREMELY PRECISE
> I'VE BEEN TOLD I'M OFTEN PRICKLY
> SO I'LL SAY PRETTY PLEASE,
> WON'T YOU START PLAYING NICE?
> OR I'LL RIP YOUR FACE OFF QUICKLY!
> I WANT IT MY WAY! I WANT IT MY WAY! I WANT IT MY WAY!

> *(Song ends. Music continues to pulse.)*

> *[MUSIC NO. 22 – "I WANT IT MY WAY" – TAG & UNDERSCORE]*

PIERCE. Relax, James, you'll give yourself a heart attack.

WHALE. My camera needs to start rolling, Mr. Pierce.

PIERCE. I'm sorry, but the make-up is all very delicate. Unless you want me to burn Boris's skin off, it'll take at least two hours to remove it and three hours to reapply what *you* want. If I hurry.

CARL. That loses the whole day. And Boris isn't called tomorrow.

PIERCE. Carl you've seen both designs. Which do you think will look better on a billboard? My way or his way?

> *(CARL thinks for a moment.)*

CARL. I'm sorry James, but I have to go with Jack on this one.

WHALE. You can't be serious. *I'm* the director.

CARL. And I'm the *producer*. You can't have your way this time. But trust me. You'll be glad once you start shooting. That green is very unusual.

WHALE. The film is in black & white!

CARL. We don't have time to redo it. It will put us behind. Now, get back down to the set and film Boris's first scene. That's my decision.

WHALE. You're going to let *him* get away with this?

CARL. I'll deal with him later. Now please...

WHALE. *(relenting)* I'll film it. But I won't be happy about it.

> **(WHALE** *exits in a huff.* **PIERCE** *beams with satisfaction.)*

CARL. Don't say a word, Jack. You're damned lucky that your design is unique and copyrightable. Whale's idea wasn't specific enough.

PIERCE. *(surprised)* Copyrightable? To me?

CARL. Don't be silly. To the studio! We own it.

PIERCE. You *own* it?

CARL. It's our movie, Jack.

PIERCE. *(concerned)* Yes...of course. I understand.

CARL. *(excited)* And I've got a feeling we'll make millions off of your work. Congratulations!

PIERCE. *(uneasy)* Uh...thank you.

CARL. Be happy. You won.

PIERCE. But you had an ulterior motive for choosing my version.

CARL. This is show *business*, Jack. Everyone has an ulterior motive. Just like you did when you switched the make-up.

PIERCE. Right.

CARL. Now I've gotta go change all of Boris's call times don't I?

PIERCE. Yes, we'll need much longer every morning.

CARL. It'll be worth it. That face is gonna be everywhere. Posters, handbills... who knows? Maybe even toys! "Universal's *Frankenstein*!"

>   *(thunder crash)*

PIERCE. It's going to take the world by storm?

CARL. Exactly!

>   (**CARL** *exits.* **PIERCE** *is practically shell-shocked as the storm continues. Music intensifies.*)

PIERCE. *(plaintively sings)*
>   I SURE GOT MY WAY!

>   *(The thunder and lightning get even stronger. Blackout.)*

>   **[MUSIC NO. 23 – TRANSITION TO ACT TWO SCENE THREE]**

Scene Three: Premiere Night
Several Months Later

(The lights restore to find **PIERCE** *and* **KARLOFF**
in the make-up room. The storm still rages as music
begins. **PIERCE** *uncorks a bottle of champagne.*
Like a mad-scientist, he carefully pours two glasses
and hands one to **KARLOFF**.*)*

[MUSIC NO. 24 – "TAKE THE WORLD BY STORM"]

KARLOFF. Here's to the opening of *Frankenstein.*

PIERCE. Or, as far as we're concerned, just another Sunday
night.

(They clink their glasses and drink.)

KARLOFF. How fitting there would be a thunderstorm
tonight.

PIERCE. This weather has been non-stop horrible for
months!

KARLOFF. Truly.

PIERCE. So how does it feel to be the star of a major motion
picture and not be invited to the premiere?

KARLOFF. Monstrous. Are you okay not being invited
either, Jack?

PIERCE. I don't care about tonight. I care about the future.
My future.

(He sings.)

I USED TO SPEND MY SUNDAYS
DISGUISING MY BEST FRIEND
MADE HIM LOOK SO DIFFERENT
I'D LOVE TO PLAY PRETEND.
THEN THE SUNDAYS TURNED TO EVERY DAY
THAT'S WHEN I KNEW
I SHOULD BECOME PART OF THE MOVIES
AND THAT'S WHAT I SWORE I'D DO!
SO I CAME HERE WITH MY KIT,
AND TO A GREAT DEGREE
I THINK THAT I'VE MADE SOMEONE FAMOUS –
BUT I DON'T MEAN ME.

'CAUSE I'M AFRAID I'LL NEVER GET THE CREDIT
I'M AFRAID THEY'LL NEVER KNOW MY NAME
BUT I DON'T WISH TO CONFORM
I WANNA TAKE THE WORLD BY STORM!
DON'T I DESERVE A LITTLE TASTE OF FAME?

> *(Music continues.)*

KARLOFF. I know how you feel, Jack. My name isn't even in the opening credits.

PIERCE. Why not?

KARLOFF. Carl wanted to keep the monster more mysterious, I suppose. I'm listed as a question mark.

PIERCE. He probably thinks it makes the producer seem like the star.

> *(He raises his glass.)*

To the monster!

> *(They clink and drink.* **VERA** *enters, wearing a fancy gown.)*

VERA. Hello boys! I saw the light on.

KARLOFF. Vera. You're all dressed up!

VERA. Oh do you like this gown? It's one of mine. I'm on my way to the premiere. I'm just heading down to wardrobe to get a raincoat.

PIERCE. How did *you* get a ticket?

VERA. Oh, I don't have a ticket. I'm just gonna stand in the crowd across the street and watch all the celebs arrive. I never miss a premiere. Sometimes they even catch me on a newsreel!

KARLOFF. Marvelous.

VERA. You can both join me if you want.

PIERCE. No, thank you.

KARLOFF. Have a wonderful time.

PIERCE. Give our regards to Carl, if you see him.

VERA. Of course. It's his big night! Bye boys.

> *(***PIERCE*** *rolls his eyes as* **VERA** *exits.)*

KARLOFF. She didn't mean it that way, Jack.

> (**PIERCE** *continues singing.*)

PIERCE.

> WHO WOULDN'T WANT THE ACCOLADES?
> WHO WOULDN'T WANT THE PRAISE?
> WHO WOULDN'T WANT THE COMPLIMENTS?
> I, AT LEAST, DESERVE A RAISE!
>
> BUT SOMEONE ELSE IS BOUND TO GET THE GLORY
> WITH MY CONTRACT, THERE'S NOT MUCH THAT I CAN DO.
> IN THIS BUSINESS, THAT'S THE NORM
> HOW CAN I TAKE THE WORLD BY STORM?
> IF I'M ONLY IN THE BACKGROUND, THEN I'M THROUGH.

> (*Music continues.*)

KARLOFF. You'll get acclaim if I have anything to say about it, Jack.

PIERCE. Thank you. And if they make a sequel, I'll demand that *both* of us to be invited to the premiere!

KARLOFF. A sequel to *Frankenstein*? Who would want the same thing all over again?

> (*Just in time to hear this,* **WHALE** *enters. He is dressed in a tux.* **PIERCE** *turns away.*)

WHALE. I wholeheartedly agree, Boris.

KARLOFF. Hello, James. Shouldn't you be on your way to the premiere?

WHALE. I can't bear the thought of you not being there, Boris.

KARLOFF. That's kind of you. But what's done is done. Carl didn't give me a ticket.

WHALE. I'm giving you *my* ticket.

KARLOFF. James, no. Then you won't be able to see your triumph.

WHALE. Boris, I've been to premieres. It's more important for *you* to be there. And I won't take no for an answer

KARLOFF. But what about Jack?

PIERCE. Don't worry about me.

WHALE. I also have something special for Jack. But you take this ticket and *go*!

> *(He hands* **KARLOFF** *the ticket.)*

KARLOFF. Do you mind, Jack?

PIERCE. Of course not. Get out of here!

KARLOFF. James, I don't know what to say.

WHALE. Say nothing. Just like in the film.

> *(***KARLOFF*** *nods and smiles as he exits.)*

PIERCE. Looks like you're a real hero tonight, James.

> *(He continues to sing as the storm keeps raging.)*

SOMEONE ALWAYS TRIES
TO STEAL MY THUNDER.
I WONDER IF I'LL EVER
GET THE CHANCE
TO FIGHT AGAINST THE EVIL,
LIKE ON SUNDAY AFTERNOONS
WHEN I USED TO KNOW THE WINNER
IN ADVANCE –

> *(***WHALE*** *interrupts him. Music continues.)*

WHALE. Could I have some of that champagne?

PIERCE. Sure.

> *(He hands him* **KARLOFF**'s *glass.* **WHALE** *drinks it down quickly. You could cut the tension with a knife.)*

WHALE. I don't think I've ever done what I'm about to do in my entire life.

PIERCE. And what's that?

WHALE. Apologize.

> *(Lightning crashes outside.)*

PIERCE. Excuse me?

WHALE. You were right about your make-up design.

PIERCE. Thank you. Though, frankly, it isn't even mine. It's the property of this place. "Copyright 1931– Universal Studios."

WHALE. That's Hollywood. But you should still be pleased with your accomplishment. It photographed... breathtakingly. The way the camera registered that green skin and those deep red scars...

PIERCE. If only the film was in color!

WHALE. Ha! Even when they perfect the technology, I doubt there will *ever* be a color horror film. Far too gruesome.

PIERCE. What do British directors know about making monster movies anyway!?

WHALE. Very amusing. Now as for tonight, I'd like you to be my guest at a private screening. A friend has managed to secure a rare print of *Nosferatu.*

PIERCE. *(surprised)* You want me to see *Nosferatu* tonight of all nights?

WHALE. Neither of us may ever get the chance again to see what horror was like in the old days.

PIERCE. I bet it's primitive.

WHALE. There's only one way to find out. Now, come on. Shall we get out of this dreadful, dreary room?

PIERCE. I'll be right behind you.

WHALE. Then I'd better watch my back!

     (**WHALE** *exits.* **PIERCE** *sings.*)

PIERCE.
    AND NOW I SPEND EACH SUNDAY
    BY THE MIRROR ON MY WALL
    TRYING NEW PROCEDURES OUT
    UNTIL I KNOW THEM ALL
    SINCE THERE'S NOTHING AS FULLFILLING
    AS CREATING ART
    AND I HOPE IF IT'S SUCCESSFUL
    THEY'LL ACKNOWLEDGE MY SMALL PART.

IF I'M LUCKY THEN AT LEAST I'LL BE REMEMBERED
AS THE MAN WHO MADE THE FACE
THAT HAUNTS YOUR SLEEP
BUT THERE ARE OTHER FILMS TO MAKE
AND THE MONSTERS CAN'T LOOK FAKE.
I HAVE TO PROVE THEIR BEAUTY'S NOT SKIN DEEP

SO IF I STAY TRUE TO MYSELF
AND IF I STAY TRUE TO FORM
I'LL REMAIN A MONSTER MAKER
AND I'LL TAKE THE WORLD BY STORM!

> *(Thunder and lightning strike. The lights focus on* **PIERCE** *as he reaches for the jar of green make-up. The rest of the stage darkens. [Scenery can begin to change.])*

I don't care what you say, Mr. James Whale. Horror should be in *color*!

> *(He holds the jar up to the light. The gray-scale make-up suddenly becomes actual green [via a light from within or a pin-spot]. He laughs maniacally as the thunder and lightning intensify outside the window. The music reaches a crescendo. Blackout.)*

[MUSIC NO. 25 – TRANSITION TO ACT THREE]

ACT THREE
"THE FINAL NAIL IN THE COFFIN"

England, 1973.
A Sound Stage At Hammer Films

(The sounds of the thunderstorm have stopped. Grand, climatic movie music begins.)

[MUSIC NO. 26 – FRANKENSTEIN MOVIE THEME]

(In the darkness we hear the voice of **PETER CUSHING** *[Actor Three] dramatically shouting.)*

PETER'S VOICE. *(as "Dr. Frankenstein")* Drown in the red blood of life you miserable creature!

> *(The lights come up on* **PETER***, revealing him as a dignified British actor in late middle-age, dressed in costume as "Dr. Frankenstein." He splashes a huge bucket of blood across an inexpensive-looking movie set that represents a desolate exterior. [This could be done with a red light flooding the stage.] The blood lands on a tarp covering the floor.* **VICTORIA** *[Actor Five], a sexy, 30-something actress stands next to him, dressed as a "Nurse" in a blonde wig. Everything is in full color, including the costumes.)*

VICTORIA. *(as a "Nurse")* No, Dr. Frankenstein!

> *(She screams bloody murder.)*

Noooooo!!!!!!

FISHER'S VOICE. And cut!

> *(Music ends. The lights reveal director* **TERENCE FISHER** *[Actor One], a somewhat petulant, energetic man in his early 40s, dressed in bell-bottomed jeans and a tye-dyed t-shirt, standing off to the side of the movie set. Flanking the set are a prop table, a make-up table with blub-lit mirror*

*and a few directors chairs. Hanging above the
set are exposed motion picture lights and sound
equipment, a boom-microphone, etc. Standing
nearby, watching the filming, is producer*
ANTHONY HINDS *[Actor Four], a jovial man in
his early 50s, wearing a leisure suit.* **FISHER** *calls
to the [unseen] camera man and crew as if they
were located past the "fourth wall.")*

FISHER. Clear *Frankenstein*. Reset for *Dracula*.

*(***PETER** *helps* **VICTORIA** *off the set.* **DRACULA'S
STUNTMAN** *[Actor Two], a nonchalant man
who is also a stagehand, enters, rolls up the blood
soaked tarp and takes it offstage.)*

VICTORIA. How was my scream, Mr. Cushing? I tried to
make it perfect.

PETER. It was extraordinary, Victoria. Nothing short of
extraordinary.

*(***VICTORIA** *smiles as* **HINDS** *approaches.)*

HINDS. Hello, Peter.

PETER. Anthony Hinds! It's been ages!

(They shake hands.)

HINDS. Been quite busy in the old office.

PETER. But you've come to the set for our last day. How
wonderful.

HINDS. I couldn't let Hammer Studios die without
attending the funeral.

PETER. Oh Anthony! I have to get to wardrobe then I'll be
right back.

*(***PETER** *exits.* **VICTORIA** *checks her make-up,
adjusts her assets in the mirror, and starts looking
over her scripts.* **FISHER** *approaches* **HINDS**.*)*

FISHER. Anthony, love, that blood isn't red enough. I need
more pigment.

HINDS. It's all we have left, Terry. It's the last jar from the
old days.

FISHER. That blood is almost twenty years old?

HINDS. The same as our plots. Can't you just light it differently in another take?

FISHER. Thanks to your budget we don't have time for another take.

HINDS. Thanks to my budget you have a job.

FISHER. Bollocks! I suppose it'll do for *Frankenstein* but you'll have to find redder blood for *Dracula* straight away.

HINDS. Where am I supposed to get it?

FISHER. I don't care if you have to drain it from the investors.

HINDS. I am afraid I already have. To the last drop.

FISHER. Whatever you have to do, love.

HINDS. You're lucky. There was a time the censors threatened to make us edit out the blood. But it certainly gave us an auspicious start.

FISHER. Yet here we are now, and I want *redder* blood. These movies are in *color*, Anthony!

HINDS. Let me put it this way: Bram Stoker and Mary Shelley won't care.

FISHER. I give up. We have to start switching the set.

(**PETER**, *now wearing a regal dressing robe, re-enters.*)

PETER. Luckily it's so Spartan, there's hardly anything to switch.

HINDS. We're gonna put in a matte painting, Peter.

FISHER. Although it may have to be painted by my twelve year old nephew.

HINDS. Terry, the budget's not *that* low.

FISHER. It remains to be seen if I can create art under these conditions!

(**DRACULA'S STUNTMAN** *has entered. Without saying a word, he approaches* **FISHER**, *ready for his next directive.*)

Get in costume and bring in the coffin!

(**DRACULA'S STUNTMAN** *nods and goes off stage as* **VICTORIA** *joins the men.*)

VICTORIA. Mr. Fisher, wasn't I supposed to remove my blouse in that scene?

FISHER. No, no, no. No exposed bosom in a *Frankenstein* movie. That would be vulgar. Only in *Dracula*. Topless in *Dracula*, love. Remember we filmed it yesterday? In your raven wig?

VICTORIA. Yes, Mr. Fisher. That's right. But I look better topless as a blonde…

FISHER. Nonsense, love. Now go change for the next scene.

VICTORIA. All right.

(*She exits.*)

FISHER. Peter, take a few minutes then we'll start shooting.

PETER. I'll be ready. Just make sure I don't start using my Dr. Frankenstein voice as Van Helsing. Or vice versa.

FISHER. Of course, love. And by the way, that last line was wrong. We'll have to loop it.

(*pointedly to* **HINDS**)

If looping's in the budget, that is.

PETER. What part was wrong?

FISHER. "Drown in the red blood of life!" is actually your line in *Dracula*. For *Frankenstein* you were supposed to say: "Drink the red blood of the living!"

PETER. Shouldn't Dracula be the one drinking the blood?

FISHER. I didn't write it, love.

PETER. I'm doing my best to create two worthy performances at the exact same time.

FISHER. Try *directing* two complete movies at the same time. I have to create two of *everything*. With the *same* everything. There's only so many angles…

(*He calls toward offstage.*)

No, no, I need the large coffin! The *large* one! Excuse me, love.

(**FISHER** *exits, leaving* **PETER** *with* **HINDS**.)

PETER. Anthony, retirement just doesn't suit you. But I'm so glad you decided to produce these last two. Albeit *simultaneously.*

HINDS. I know it's not ideal. But we wanted to give the world a final pair of Peter Cushing Hammer horror movies.

PETER. I fancied doing them very much. But, I think the world could have lived with just one.

HINDS. We only had the total budget for *one* film, but half the investors wanted a *Frankenstein* and half insisted on *Dracula.* No one would budge. So the only way to make it feasible was to go back and forth and re-use the sets, or lose the funding entirely.

PETER. How frightful! Don't tell Terry, but yesterday I did an entire Dr. Frankenstein scene wearing my Van Helsing suit.

HINDS. That wouldn't have happened in the '50s, my friend.

> (**VICTORIA** *enters wearing a very short, skimpy, satin dressing robe.*)

VICTORIA. Sorry, I forgot my stockings.

> (*She gets them from the make-up table.*)

PETER. That's all right, dear. You must be looking forward to staying in *one* set of clothes all day once we've wrapped.

VICTORIA. Not really.

> (*She rushes off.* **PETER** *turns to* **HINDS.**)

PETER. *Nothing* in the '70s would have happened in the '50s.

HINDS. Back then we wouldn't even dream of showing skin in a picture. Today I can hardly get one financed without it.

PETER. At least we've come a long way from stealing… cashing in on Universal's successes.

HINDS. Undeniably! Where would we be without the public domain?

PETER. I was hoping that we could have finally used that famous original make-up for the monster. Wouldn't Universal finally give in after all these years? All these sequels?

HINDS. They're *still* protecting the copyright on Karloff's face. And they said they'd sue for infringement if we even make him green.

PETER. Dear Boris, may he rest in peace. He'd have wanted us to use it.

HINDS. The studio owns it and they won't even consider licensing that make-up by whatever-his-name-was.

PETER. Oh yes. Boris used to rave about the man who designed the look. Couldn't *we* have hired what's-his-name?

HINDS. From America? Would you have paid for it?

PETER. I might have.

HINDS. I think he died years ago. But he did do a lot of the monsters back in the heyday.

PETER. Well, whoever he was, he'd probably never have adapted to our working conditions. It's certainly not Hollywood.

HINDS. Hollywood's not Hollywood anymore, Peter. All the public wants today is *Rosemary's Baby... The Exorcist...*

PETER. Not *our* kind of Horror.

HINDS. Who would've ever believed that Frankenstein and Dracula's ultimate killer would be society itself?

PETER. I always hoped these movies couldn't be killed.

HINDS. Well, we always found some crazy way to bring Dracula back to life, didn't we?

PETER. I only wish Chris was in this one. Isn't there anything you could have done to get him to play Dracula one last time for our devoted fans?

HINDS. I tried. But you know he's been swearing that he's through playing the vampire for the last four sequels.

PETER. How true.

HINDS. I promised him it was *definitely* the grand finale. But this time he kept his word.

PETER. So you cast his stuntman as Dracula? Really, Anthony.

HINDS. He was cheap. And he's also a stage-hand.

> *(As they talk,* **DRACULA'S STUNTMAN,** *now dressed in a complete Dracula costume, drags a large coffin onto the set, then goes back offstage.)*

It kills three birds.

PETER. There's only one Dracula and that's Christopher Lee.

HINDS. That's what they used to say about Lugosi.

PETER. Try acting with "Dracula's Stuntman."

HINDS. At least he didn't complain when we cut all his lines.

PETER. I'm sure he was relieved. He always skulks around like he's in his own private silent movie anyway.

HINDS. I've seen the rushes and the back of his head looks a lot like Chris. And he's simply smashing in the cape… from behind.

PETER. But he's not even a good *growler.*

HINDS. Just one more day with him, then you'll be done with Dracula forever, Peter.

PETER. But I don't want to be *done* with Dracula. I just want to Dracula to be Chris.

HINDS. Why have *you* always agreed to keep doing these low-budget fright flicks?

PETER. I adore them.

HINDS. But an actor of your stature…

PETER. They may not have been in the original vision for my résumé. But these films bring joy to many people.

HINDS. At least they used to!

PETER. Audiences will be sorry when they're gone.

HINDS. Hasn't it bothered you, that over the years the quality went…well…downward?

PETER. Not at all…

> *(Music begins.)*

> **[MUSIC NO. 27 – "NEVER LET THE PERFECT BE THE ENEMY OF THE GOOD"]**

> *(He sings.)*

I NEVER LET THE PERFECT
BE THE ENEMY OF THE GOOD
I NEVER SAY I SHOULDN'T
EVEN IF I THINK SHOULD
I SEE THE GLASS HALF FULL
NO REASON NOT TO DRINK
I'M HAPPY DOING HORROR
I DON'T CARE WHAT CRITICS THINK!

> *(Music continues.*

> **FISHER** *enters with* **DRACULA'S STUNTMAN,** *who carries on the actor's extra costume pieces and places them near the film set.)*

HINDS. I'd better get back to the office, but I'll be here for the last scene. Good luck.

FISHER. Actors on the set, please!

> *(***HINDS*** *exits.*

> **VICTORIA,** *now in a raven-haired wig, costumed in a negligee as a "Bride of Dracula," enters and takes her place.*

> **PETER** *moves to the set.)*

Peter don't fall in the coffin!

> *(***PETER*** *narrowly avoids the coffin and continues to sing.)*

PETER.

WHEN I WAS FILMING DRAMAS
FOR THE BBC
THEY KNEW THE WAY TO
GET THE BEST PERFORMANCE OUT OF ME

WAS NOT TO MAKE A PROMISE
THAT THEY COULD NOT FULFILL
I KNEW IT WASN'T HOLLYWOOD
WITH MILLIONS IN THE TILL.

> (*Music continues.* **FISHER** *speaks to the cameraman again as if he were beyond the "fourth wall."*)

FISHER. Okay, we need to get these in *one* take. We're doing master shots first. Peter, on your mark please, love.

> (**PETER** *removes the dressing robe to reveal his "Van Helsing" suit and goes to the set.* **DRACULA'S STUNTMAN** *"claps" a clapboard.*)

Action.

> (*The lights narrow in on the film set, which is not much more than the coffin in a darkened room. Music continues.*)

PETER. *(as "Van Helsing")* Where is Count Dracula?

VICTORIA. *(as "Bride of Dracula")* My husband is out drinking. Now give me your neck!

> (*She bears her fangs and hisses.* **PETER** *as "Van Helsing" makes the sign of the cross with his fingers.*)

FISHER. And cut! Re-set for *Frankenstein.* And wardrobe. Hurry! Hurry!

> (*Music continues. Lights restore to full stage.* **VICTORIA** *steps off the set and promptly strips down to her underthings [which can be extremely revealing, or a more modest camisole and slip] and changes costume in full view of everyone – she's not shy.* **PETER** *tries not to look.* **FISHER** *switches scripts.* **DRACULA'S STUNTMAN** *quickly pushes the coffin off the set while bringing on a huge piece of lab equipment, nearly hitting* **PETER** *in the process.*)

Don't hit Peter with that thing!

(PETER ducks and moves out of the way. He continues to sing as the set is re-dressed.)

PETER.

I NEVER LET THE PERFECT
BE THE ENEMY OF THE GOOD
THERE'S NOTHING WRONG WITH
SETTLING
I WISH MORE PEOPLE WOULD
OF COURSE I HAVE MY STANDARDS
MY NAME'S ON THAT MARQUEE.
BUT THE BUSINESS IS FOR OTHERS
I JUST STAY CONCERNED WITH ME!

(PETER struggles to unfasten his "Van Helsing" trousers. FISHER calls to DRACULA'S STUNTMAN.)

FISHER. Help Peter change his costume. Get those bloody trousers off him!

(DRACULA'S STUNTMAN pulls down PETER's trousers, revealing boxer shorts and support stockings with garters. PETER maintains his dignity as he changes into his "Dr. Frankenstein" trousers and gothic lab-coat – all while continuing to sing.)

PETER.

SINCE I KNOW WHAT I'M DOING
I KNOW MY EVERY MARK AND LINE
I STAY HOPEFUL THAT THE
FINAL PRODUCT
WILL SHINE
AND NOT DECLINE
BUT NO MATTER HOW IT GOES... IT'S FINE!

(Music continues.)

FISHER. Peter, on your mark. Victoria, off camera.

(The lights narrow in on the film set, which is not much more than a large piece of electrical equipment in a darkened room. PETER and VICTORIA take

their places. **DRACULA'S STUNTMAN** *"claps" a clapboard.)*

FISHER. Action.

(**VICTORIA** *runs onto the set, having forgotten to switch her wig. Music continues.)*

VICTORIA. *(as "Nurse")* Dr. Frankenstein, the monster has escaped from the...

FISHER. *(calling)* Wig!

VICTORIA. *(as herself)* What?

FISHER. Wig! Keep rolling. Victoria, you forgot to switch your wig!

(**DRACULA'S STUNTMAN** *comes up from behind and swaps the raven wig with the blonde one.)*

VICTORIA. I'm so sorry. I wanted to be perfect.

PETER. Don't apologize dear, it's all part of the fun.

FISHER. Again. From your line, Victoria. Action!

VICTORIA. *(as "Nurse")* Dr. Frankenstein, the monster has escaped from the laboratory. He's heading for the village!

PETER. *(as "Dr. Frankenstein")* I never much cared for that village anyway!

(He finishes with a big hand gesture.)

FISHER. And cut!

(Lights restore.)

Peter, do me a favor, love, and stay completely frozen while we reposition the camera.

(**PETER** *tries to not move, though caught in an awkward pose.)*

Get ready for close-ups. Victoria, you're off.

(**VICTORIA** *moves off the set.* **PETER**'s *raised arm starts to waver.)*

I need you *completely* still, Peter!

(**PETER** *does his best as he continues to sing.)*

PETER.

> WHEN I WAS PLAYING SHERLOCK
> AND EVEN DOCTOR WHO
> I REALIZED THEY WERE CHARACTERS
> THE PUBLIC CLEARLY KNEW.
> AND I WOULD BE COMPARED
> PERHAPS UNFAIRLY SO.
> I COULDN'T LET IT GET TO ME
> I JUST MAINTAINED THE STATUS QUO!

> *(Music continues.* **DRACULA'S STUNTMAN**
> *"claps" a clapboard.)*

FISHER. Action.

> *(The lights narrow in on the film set even more
> extremely – to suggest a close-up.* **VICTORIA** *runs
> onto the set.)*

VICTORIA. *(as "Nurse")* Dr. Frankenstein, the monster has escaped from the laboratory. He's heading for the village!

PETER. *(as "Dr. Frankenstein")* I never much cared for that village anyway!

> *(same big gesture)*

FISHER. And cut! Bring back the coffin. Strike the lab. And wardrobe! Hurry! Hurry!

> *(Music continues. Lights widen. It's near chaos.*
> **VICTORIA** *swaps out her wig and changes clothes
> in front of everyone again.* **PETER** *changes his
> own trousers this time.* **FISHER** *switches his scripts.*
> **DRACULA'S STUNTMAN** *quickly pushes the coffin
> back onto the set.* **PETER** *is careful to avoid it this
> time.* **DRACULA'S STUNTMAN** *then disconnects
> an electrical cord from the lab equipment.* **FISHER**
> *calls to him.)*

That's a live wire! Don't let it electrocute Peter!

> *(***PETER*** *soldiers on, practically afraid to move)*

PETER.

    I NEVER LET THE PERFECT
    BE THE ENEMY OF THE GOOD
    THERE'S NOTHING WRONG WITH
    SECOND BEST
    THAT'S ALWAYS WHERE I STOOD.
    IT DOESN'T MEAN GIVE UP
    THE OPPOSITE IS TRUE
    I RELAX AND LET MY INSTINCTS
    DO THE THINGS THEY ALWAYS DO!

        (**FISHER** *calls to* **PETER** *as* **DRACULA'S STUNTMAN** *prepares the set.*)

FISHER. Don't worry if the left wall falls over, we're only shooting the right.

        (**PETER** *instinctively moves away from the wall and continues to sing as he puts on his suit jacket.*)

PETER.

    IN MY FIRST FILM AT HAMMER
    AS DOCTOR FRANKENSTEIN
    WE DIDN'T HAVE RESOURCES
    HALF THE CLOTHES I WORE WERE MINE!
    THEN DRACULA CAME AFTER
    AND FUNDS WERE JUST AS TIGHT
    THEY BOTH BECAME BIG HITS
    AND NOT BECAUSE OF WHAT WE HAD –
    BUT IN SPITE!

        (**PETER** *moves to his mark.* **FISHER** *calls out.*)

FISHER. Are we sure that equipment hanging over Peter's head is secure?

        (**PETER** *takes a nervous peek above him, wipes the sweat from his brow, and bravely keeps singing.*)

PETER.

    YES, I KNOW WHAT I'M DOING
    I KNOW MY EVERY MARK AND LINE
    I STAY HOPEFUL THAT THE
    FINAL PRODUCT

WILL SHINE
AND NOT DECLINE
BUT NO MATTER HOW IT GOES... IT'S FINE!

>   *(Music continues.)*

FISHER. Now remember this is a tight close-up, Peter. Let me see it in your eyes.

>   (**DRACULA'S STUNTMAN** *"claps" the clapboard.*)

Action.

>   *(The lights narrow in on the film set again, suggesting a close-up.)*

PETER. *(as "Van Helsing")* Where is Count Dracula?

VICTORIA. *(as "Bride of Dracula")* My husband is out drinking. Now give me your neck!

>   *(She bears her fangs and hisses.* **PETER** *as "Van Helsing" makes the sign of the cross with his fingers.* **FISHER** *interrupts them.)*

FISHER. Hold please. There's a shadow across Victoria's chest.

PETER. *(sarcastic)* Oh no, we have to be able to see them.

>   (**VICTORIA** *tries to "adjust" herself.)*

FISHER. Keep rolling. No one move.

>   *(He calls toward the "fourth wall.")*

Lads, can we adjust that?

>   *(While holding completely still,* **PETER** *slowly sings.)*

PETER.

SO NOW I'M LOOKING BACK
ON A WONDERFUL CAREER
IF I DIDN'T WANT TO DO THIS
I WOULD SURELY NOT BE HERE
ALTHOUGH I THINK MY PUBLIC
JUST MIGHT HAVE UNDERSTOOD –

FISHER. No, don't worry about the light on Peter, we're just zooming in on Victoria's cleavage.

(**PETER** *grits his teeth and keeps singing.*)

PETER.
BUT I NEVER LET THE PERFECT
BE THE ENEMY OF THE GOOD!

(*Music intensifies as it draws to a climax.*)

FISHER. Okay, one last time, bear your fangs and hiss, Victoria.

(*While sticking out her chest, she hisses wetly –
right in* **PETER***'s face.*)

PETER.
OH NO, I NEVER LET THE PERFECT
BE THE ENEMY –
OF THE GOOD!

(*Music crescendos as the lights begin to widen.*)

FISHER. And cut!

(*The music ends with a flourish.*)

Well done. Everyone take a break, while we re-set for the final scene.

(**VICTORIA** *removes her wig.* **PETER** *puts his dressing robe back on.*)

PETER. How exhilarating! Remind me what's left.

FISHER. *Frankenstein's* a wrap. We just need to film you killing Dracula. Look over the lines. Or make them up. Whichever you prefer, love.

(*He turns to* **DRACULA'S STUNTMAN**.*)

We need to move the coffin to the opposite side.

(**HINDS** *solemnly enters carrying a cardboard box of various items – as if he has cleaned out his office.*)

HINDS. There won't be any need for that.

PETER. Anthony, you look white as a ghost. What's wrong?

HINDS. I'm afraid filming is cancelled.

FISHER. What?

PETER. What do you mean?

HINDS. I just got off the wire with our distributors. They found out that Chris isn't playing Dracula.

PETER. *(shocked)* You hadn't told them?

HINDS. *(sheepishly)* I was hoping they wouldn't mind.

FISHER. So what have they done?

HINDS. They've refused to send over the balance of their distribution fee. And without it we can't continue.

> *(They are all stunned. Even* **DRACULA'S STUNTMAN**.*)*

PETER. But...what about...

HINDS. They aren't interested in a *Frankenstein* picture without a *Dracula* picture and they aren't interested in a *Dracula* picture without Christopher Lee.

PETER. Peter Cushing isn't enough?

HINDS. It's not that, Peter. Of course they want you too. It's just...

PETER. They don't want Cushing without Lee.

HINDS. Well...

> *(***PETER*** is crushed, but tries to put on a brave face.)*

PETER. Do I at least I get *half* the credit for our successes?

HINDS. It's not like that, Peter.

PETER. Chris plays the monster. The vampire. Of course he's more popular. I'm just the one who tries to destroy him. And now I don't even get a triumph of my own.

HINDS. Peter...

PETER. Maybe I could talk Chris into coming down here and we could splice him into a few scenes.

> *(He turns to* **DRACULA'S STUNTMAN**.*)*

Sorry, no offense, old boy.

> *(***DRACULA'S STUNTMAN*** shrugs.)*

HINDS. I thought of that. But he's in the States talking over a picture offer with Universal Studios.

FISHER. Universal? The house of horror has lured him away.

PETER. *This* is the house of horror.

HINDS. Indeed.

FISHER. But *we're* all here now and we only have one scene left to film. Can't we just finish and then try to find new distributors?

HINDS. It's too late. There's no money left in the coffers. We have to return the unused cans of film and beg for a refund.

FISHER. But, if we...

HINDS. Terry, we can't even afford to develop the negatives...or pay the crew for the rest of the day. I wasted too much damned money on the posters.

PETER. You printed the posters before we even finished?

HINDS. Before we even *started*. That was always our system. It's best to have the poster early to get people excited in advance. See, look how exciting!

> *(He pulls a poster out of his box and unrolls it to reveal garish double-feature artwork.)*

PETER. *(reading)* "Frankenstein's Brother!" and "Stake the Heart of Dracula!"

> *(He looks puzzled.)*

HINDS. Don't you like the titles?

PETER. I suppose there's a certain...dramatic ring to them.

HINDS. They were better than *Frankenstein Seven* and *Dracula Nine*.

PETER. But I don't recall Frankenstein even having a brother in the script.

FISHER. You were *playing* Dr. Frankenstein's brother.

PETER. No one told me.

HINDS. The distributors liked the titles, so we just dusted off some old spec scripts that were close enough. We'd have looped in narration explaining who you were.

PETER. How...clever.

HINDS. It's all rubbish now.

FISHER. It can't end like this, Anthony.

HINDS. I'm afraid it has.

VICTORIA. *(sadly)* This was my big break.

HINDS. Victoria, darling, you have a brilliant career ahead of you in...*other* kinds of films.

VICTORIA. But I wanted to do *these.*

HINDS. Peter, I don't know what to say.

PETER. There's nothing to say. I understand the situation. Sometimes show business is unkind.

HINDS. Chin up, my friend. I should go see if I can negotiate to sell off some of our equipment.

> *(He starts to exit, but turns back.)*

I'm terribly sorry that I let this happen. But I suppose I didn't want our party to end. Now look what I've done. I should have stayed in retirement.

> *(He exits.* **VICTORIA** *starts removing her costume and changing into her own mini-dress. Music begins.)*

> *[MUSIC NO. 28 – "NAIL IN THE COFFIN"]*

FISHER. That bastard!

PETER. Now Terry, we'll have none of that.

FISHER. *(angry)* Peter... *Two* unfinished films.

PETER. I know, Terry. I know...

> *(He sings.)*

IT'S THE FINAL NAIL IN THE COFFIN!
HOW SHOCKING IT'S ENDING THIS WAY.

FISHER.

THE FINAL NAIL IN THE COFFIN
IT'S NOT FAIR BEING BURIED TODAY.

PETER.

> THE FINAL NAIL IN THE COFFIN
>
> AFTER YEARS OF… WELL… *SEMI* RENOWN

FISHER.

> THE FINAL NAIL IN THE COFFIN
>
> NOW THE HAMMER HAS FINALLY COME DOWN.

PETER.

> SINCE OUR LEGACY ISN'T SECURE NOW –

FISHER.

> OUR PRIDE AND OUR BLOOD ALL BUT DRAINED…

PETER.

> – I'M SORRY I WASN'T MORE FAMOUS.

FISHER.

> I'M SORRY I EVER COMPLAINED.

> *(They move to comfort each other.)*

PETER & FISHER.

> NOW THE FINAL MAN WITH THE SHOVEL
>
> HAS CREPT UP BEHIND US TOO FAST
>
> SO WE MUST CLOSE THE LID ON OUR FUTURE
>
> AND WE MUST MARK THE GRAVE OF OUR PAST.

PETER.

> I FEAR THERE MAY BE NO MORE OFFERS
>
> IF ONE CONSIDERS MY AGE

FISHER.

> AND IF I'M WASHED UP IN THE MOVIES…

PETER.

> …YOU COULD ALWAYS DIRECT FOR THE STAGE!

FISHER. No, love, no!

PETER.

> THE FINAL NECK HAS BEEN BITTEN!
>
> THE MONSTER HAS FALLEN APART!

FISHER.

> WE DIDN'T DO THIS FOR MONEY –

PETER.

> WE DID IT FOR ART.

PETER & FISHER.
>IT'S THE FINAL NAIL IN THE COFFIN
>SO WE'LL PUT BACK THE FANGS AND THE CAPE
>AND WE'LL TURN OFF THE LIGHTS IN THE DUNGEON
>FOR A LESS THAN HEROIC ESCAPE.

PETER.
>THE FINAL NAIL IN THE COFFIN...

FISHER.
>WITH HARDLY A MOMENT TO GRIEVE –

PETER.
>AFTER YEARS OF HORRIFIC ADVENTURES...
>I'M AFRAID IT'S IMPOSSIBLE TO LEAVE!

>*(Music ends.* **FISHER** *pats* **PETER** *on the shoulder and then addresses* **DRACULA'S STUNTMAN**.*)*

FISHER. Come on, love, we'd better start clearing the stage.

>*(He calls toward the fourth wall.)*

You blokes can start striking the gear.

>*(***FISHER** *and* **DRACULA'S STUNTMAN** *exit as* **VICTORIA**, *now dressed, nervously approaches* **PETER**.)*

VICTORIA. Mr. Cushing?

PETER. You don't have to call me Mr. Cushing.

VICTORIA. Well... I've been trying to get my nerve to chat with you since the day we started filming. Now it looks like this is my last chance.

PETER. What is it dear?

VICTORIA. When I got these parts, it was the most extraordinary thing to ever happen to me...

PETER. How exciting.

>*(Bright 1970s "Bacharach" style music begins.)*

>*[MUSIC NO. 29 – "HORROR FAN"]*

VICTORIA. Yes. You see, my earliest memory is being taken to an old German vampire movie in a small festival outside London. I don't remember what it was called, but I know there wasn't any talking. And I always watched those old black & white films from Hollywood on the telly. And then, of course, I saw all your original Hammer pictures. What I'm trying to say is, I'm not *just* an actress...

   (She sings.)

MISTER ... MONSTER MAN,
I'M A HORROR FAN!
EVERY MATINEE...
EVERY SINGLE WEEK
IN THE DARKNESS
I WOULD WATCH THE SCREEN AND SWOON
WHILE THE REST WOULD SHRIEK!

PETER. How lovely.

   (VICTORIA *moves closer to really press her point.*
   PETER *does his best to pay attention to her words,*
   not her chest.)

VICTORIA.

MISTER MONSTER MAN
I'M A HORROR FAN
I WOULD ASK MY MUM
IF SHE'D TAKE ME THERE
TO THE PICTURE SHOW
EACH WEEKEND AFTERNOON
WHERE I'D GET MY SCARE

ON A DOUBLE BILL
WERE YOU AND MISTER LEE.
AND SOMETIMES VINCENT PRICE
WOULD MAKE IT THREE.
MY CHUMS WOULD FOCUS ON THEIR CLOTHES
AND THEIR HAIR AND NOT MUCH MORE.
WHILE I WAS BUSY WATCHING BLOOD AND GORE.

AT EACH FILM DEBUT...
I WAS IN THE QUEUE

MISTER MONSTER MAN,
I'M A HORROR FAN

MY ENTIRE LIFE...
NOW I'M HERE WITH YOU.
EVEN THOUGH IT MY BE OVER MUCH TOO SOON.
STILL MY WISH CAME TRUE
MISTER MONSTER MAN,
I'M A HORROR FAN...
I'M A HORROR FAN...
I'M A HORROR FAN!

> *(She impulsively hugs him as the song ends.)*

PETER. That simply means the world to me, dear. Thank you.

VICTORIA. There's millions like me, Mr. Cushing. And we need you. Monster movies are...*essential.*

PETER. *(touched)* Victoria, you said the magic words.

> **(HINDS** *enters.)*

HINDS. I just sold Frankenstein's laboratory to Oxford.

PETER. They realize it's not a *real* laboratory I hope.

HINDS. To their theatre department.

PETER. I'm glad you're here.

> *(He calls offstage.)*

Could I have everyone's attention please?

> **(FISHER** *and* **DRACULA'S STUNTMAN** *enter.)*

HINDS. What is it, Peter?

PETER. Victoria has helped me make an important decision.

VICTORIA. I have?

PETER. Terry, I'd like you to please put everything back in place for the final scene of *Dracula.*

HINDS. Peter, we can't.

PETER. We can if I give you back my compensation.

> *(They all gasp in surprise.)*

HINDS. What?

PETER. My fee. I want to give it back. Invest it in the pictures to be precise.

FISHER. Are you serious, love?

PETER. I've never been more serious in my life.

HINDS. I can't let you...

PETER. Oh yes you can. This is what I want – more than anything in the world. Neither Dr. Frankenstein nor Professor Van Helsing is going to let the evil nemesis win just yet.

HINDS. Peter...

PETER. I'm going to write you a check to cover the rest of the filming and editing costs. And once you have two completed pictures, you can worry about finding another distributor. For heaven's sake *someone* will want them.

HINDS. With any luck.

> (**FISHER** *excitedly wastes no time in getting everything back together. He calls to* **DRACULA'S STUNTMAN**.)

FISHER. Put the coffin back.

> (**DRACULA'S STUNTMAN** *starts moving the coffin back onto the set.* **FISHER** *calls to the "fourth wall."*)

Get the camera back in position.

HINDS. Peter, I'm truly touched that you would do this for me.

PETER. Oh, Anthony, I love you dearly, but it's not for you. Or for Hammer.

> (*He turns to* **VICTORIA**.)

It's for the "essential" art of the classic monster movie.

> (*He squeezes her hand.*)

And for my biggest horror fan.

VICTORIA. Oh Mr. Cushing...

> (*She hugs him.*)

I'd better get these clothes off!

(She starts stripping and putting her costume back on. PETER turns to HINDS.)

PETER. There's still a little life left in these old monsters, Anthony!

HINDS. There is *now*. But just because you're paying for them, don't expect to own the copyright on the films, Peter.

PETER. *(laughing)* How generous!

FISHER. Okay, let's get to it! On set everyone.

(PETER, VICTORIA and DRACULA'S STUNTMAN move to the set. PETER takes off his dressing robe as VICTORIA finishes changing and checking her make-up. DRACULA'S STUNTMAN hands PETER a special-effect blood packet, which he rigs. HINDS watches at the side.)

HINDS. Make this shot count, Terry.

FISHER. You know I will, love.

HINDS. That Peter Cushing is the finest gentleman there is. He knew what was at stake…

FISHER. Oh, that reminds me.

(FISHER goes to the prop table and grabs a sharp wooden stake.)

We can't forget this!

HINDS. Of course not.

(FISHER places it on the set.)

FISHER. Everybody ready?

PETER. Ready.

VICTORIA. Wait, my wig!

(DRACULA'S STUNTMAN hands her the dark wig and helps her put it on.)

All right, ready!

(The lights focus in on the movie set.)

FISHER. Then let's do this.

(*He addresses* **DRACULA'S STUNTMAN.**)

FISHER. Remember, only let the camera see the back of your head.

(**DRACULA'S STUNTMAN** *wryly turns his back to* **FISHER**, *claps the clapboard, tosses it off the set and takes his place inside the coffin.* **FISHER** *calls out.*)

FISHER. Action!

(*Underscore music begins.*)

[MUSIC NO. 30 – "DRACULA MOVIE THEME"]

(*In the scene,* **VICTORIA** *holds* **PETER** *by the neck.*)

VICTORIA. (*as "Bride of Dracula"*) Professor Van Helsing, you must now surrender to my husband, Count Dracula.

PETER. (*as "Van Helsing"*) Over my dead body!

VICTORIA. (*as "Bride of Dracula"*) Precisely!

(**PETER** *pushes her away, then pulls out a crucifix on a chain around his neck and holds it to her face. She hisses, screams, squirms and finally falls to the ground, dead.*

DRACULA'S STUNTMAN *finally gets to perform his stunt. He jumps out of the coffin in one swift move, with the cape flowing behind him, and his back to the camera.*

Underscore music intensifies. The lights narrow in. "Dracula" runs toward **PETER**/*"Van Helsing" and they battle.* **PETER** *reaches for the stake and finally grabs it.*)

PETER. (*as "Van Helsing"*) You'll never stop me, Dracula!

(*"Dracula" hisses and growls. They continue to battle. "Dracula" gets hold of the sharp stake and starts slashing at* **PETER**/*"Van Helsing." Finally it cuts him.*)

FISHER. Cue effect.

(**PETER** *releases the blood packet. Blood starts gushing from his wound. When "Dracula" sees the blood, he goes crazy and lunges for it, dropping the stake. Music goes wild.* **PETER**/*"Van Helsing" gets hold of the stake, and as "Dracula" attempts to lick at the blood, he pushes him into the coffin and plunges the stake into his heart.*)

PETER. *(as "Van Helsing")* Now, drown in the red blood of life!!!

(*He allows the blood from his wound to drip down onto "Dracula" then slams the coffin shut. Music Ends.*)

FISHER. And cut! Beautiful Peter.

(*Lights restore.* **FISHER** *and* **HINDS** *applaud him.*)

PETER. *Perfect*, Victoria.

(**VICTORIA** *stands up and hugs him.* **FISHER** *and* **HINDS** *join them as* **PETER** *wipes the fake blood on towel.*)

HINDS. *(emotional)* I guess that does it then.

FISHER. It's a wrap!

HINDS. I think you've truly fulfilled your destiny, Peter.

PETER. What do you mean?

HINDS. You've spent nearly two decades doing it on the screen, but now by paying for the films, you've finally become a "monster maker" in *real life*!

PETER. I suppose I have indeed.

(**PETER** *smiles and proudly looks at the surroundings.*)

How terrifying!

(*They all chuckle. Music begins.* **PETER** *sings.*)

[*MUSIC NO. 31 – "NAIL IN THE COFFIN" – REPRISE*]

IT'S THE FINAL NAIL IN THE COFFIN
THE FINAL CREATURE ATTACK
AND THOUGH HE HAS MADE MANY MONSTERS

DOCTOR FRANKENSTEIN'S NOT COMING BACK
THE FINAL NAIL IN THE COFFIN
THE FINAL BLOODY GOODBYE
AFTER SO MANY SEQUELS AND REMAKES,
IT'S FINALLY TIME FOR
DRACULA TO DIE!

(PETER stands triumphantly atop the coffin. Music swells as the lights narrow in on the small group. They hug and congratulate each other.

Finally, from the coffin comes a loud knocking sound. DRACULA'S STUNTMAN is still inside!

We hear his muffled voice at last.)

DRACULA'S STUNTMAN. *(voice)* Hey, can someone let me out of this coffin?

(PETER steps off the coffin and moves forward into a pool of light as the rest of the stage darkens behind him. The music changes for the epilogue...)

EPILOGUE
"THE END!?"

[MUSIC NO. 32 – "FINALE"]

(PETER sings.)

PETER.

DON'T EVER LET THE PERFECT
BE THE ENEMY OF THE GOOD...

(PIERCE enters from the darkness into his own pool of light. He sings.)

PIERCE.

IF YOU'RE CREATING A MONSTER,
YOU MUST GIVE THE MONSTER RESPECT...

(Finally, MURNAU enters from the darkness into a pool of light. He sings.)

MURNAU.

PLEASE DON'T SACRIFICE YOUR VISION.
NO MATTER WHO THE DEMONS ARE
THAT YOU MAY HAVE TO FIGHT!

(They each strike a final pose as the music crescendos. Blackout.)

[MUSIC NO. 33 – BOWS/EXIT MUSIC]

The End

AUTHOR'S BIOGRAPHY

Stephen Dolginoff (Book, Music & Lyrics) received Drama Desk Award nominations for Best Musical & Best Music; an Outer Critics Circle Award nomination for Best Off-Broadway musical; and won an ASCAP Music Award for his musical THRILL ME: THE LEOPOLD & LOEB STORY. More than 100 productions in 15 countries and 10 languages have followed, including a run on London's West End (WOS Award nom), productions in Los Angeles and Chicago, and long-running Asian versions in Seoul, Tokyo and China. Stephen's musical suspense thriller, FLAMES, has been seen in London and across the USA. His horror-movie musical homage, MONSTER MAKERS, was first presented at the Daryl Roth Theatre/D-Lounge by New York Theatre Barn, followed by productions around the world. Stephen received a Backstage Bistro Award for Outstanding Book, Music & Lyrics for his musical ONE FOOT OUT THE DOOR. His musical MOST MEN ARE; his musical adaptation of JOURNEY TO THE CENTER OF THE EARTH; and his musical comedy, PANIC – the story behind the "War of the Worlds" broadcast – have all been performed in theatres throughout the country. Stephen received a BFA in Dramatic Writing from NYU/Tisch School of the Arts. His work is published by Samuel French and Dramatists Play Service. As an actor, he played "Nathan Leopold" in THRILL ME Off-Broadway and on the cast album; and originated the roles of "Max Schreck," "Boris Karloff" and "Peter Cushing" in MONSTER MAKERS onstage and on the original cast recording. Visit www.stephendolginoff.com